The Mystery Hunters
at the Haunted Lodge

by

I0539593

Capwell Wyckoff

IAEGCA

**Portuguese Institute of Higher Studies in Geopolitics
and Auxiliary Sciences**

Lisbon, 2014

Title:
The Mystery Hunters at the Haunted Lodge

Author:
Capwell Wyckoff

Copyright:
Public Domain
This Edition © IAEGCA

Cover Design:
The Saalfield Publishing Company

Book Design:
Flávio Gonçalves

ISBN:
978-989-99294-5-6

Publishers:
IAEGCA
Flávio Gonçalves

Contact:
iaegca@gmail.com
http://www.geopol.com.pt
/iaegca

Printed in the United States of America and in the European Union

The Mystery Hunters
at the Haunted Lodge

by

Capwell Wyckoff

www.geopol.com.pt

**Portuguese Institute of Higher Studies in Geopolitics
and Auxiliary Sciences**

ÍNDICE

CAPWELL WYCKOFF

CHAPTER I
The Mystery Hunters

The High School at Cloverfield was quiet as the hands of the clock approached the three-o'clock hour. Then a gong pealed out and the building became a very beehive of sound. The thump of many feet and the hum of voices was heard. Healthy, wholesome young boys and girls poured out of the side doors and swarmed over the campus. Overcoats were pulled tighter as the nip of the keen Vermont air was encountered.

Two boys had come out together, and they paused to wait for two others. The boy with the clean-cut, manly face and the sparkling eyes was Barry Garrison, an outstanding boy in the Cloverfield High School. He had been the right halfback on the school team this year and had helped to lead it to a glorious record of no defeats and first place on the Conference list. He was an all-around athlete and stood well in his senior-year studies. Although Barry Garrison would have turned the idea aside with a good-natured laugh, he was the most popular boy in the high school.

His lifelong chum was Kent Marple. Kent's father owned the local hotel, and the boy had enjoyed many advantages in life. He and Barry had been friends ever since they had been small boys. Young Marple was broader than Barry, with a heavy shock of black hair and a chin that was a trifle determined. He had played fullback on the football team during the past season.

These two boys did not seem to be in any hurry. Barry leaned against a maple tree and whistled softly, while Kent glanced from one side door of the school to the other.

"The twins must have been kept in," Barry observed.

"Maybe they are clapping erasers for the teacher," Kent grinned.

"If they are, they'll clap 'em clean," Barry laughed. "The Ford twins always finish what they start. Here they come now."

Two boys came springing down the steps of the school building and looked around for Barry and Kent. When they had seen their particular friends, one of them waved, and then both boys dashed across the hard ground toward the boys under the trees. At first glance there was little to distinguish between Mac and Tim Ford. They were both the same height and build, stocky young fellows who had made splendid ends on the team. But at closer range some differences were apparent. Mac was sandy-haired, and Tim was gifted with a light brown mass of hair that sometimes managed to stay combed. Both boys had attractive, lively countenances and were well liked by everyone in the small town. They were often the leaders in the fun and could always be counted on to join in any kind of a lark. With Kent and Barry, they made up a quartet that was widely known.

Mac Ford beat his brother to the maple tree by a yard. "Thought we never would get out," he panted. "Took Tim's advice in a problem, and it was wrong. Had to do it over."

"The trouble is that you *didn't* take my advice," Tim denied. "I tried to show you how to work it, but——"

"Never mind," Barry interposed, thrusting his hands deep into his sweater pockets. "Let's move along. It's cold today."

"It ought to be," Kent observed. "Christmas is almost here."

Two high-school boys and a girl passed them and nodded and smiled. "There they go," the girl cried. "The mystery hunters!"

"Four Sherlocks, the locker-room detectives!" chimed in one of the boys. When this trio had passed on, the four chums looked at one another.

"They seem to keep calling us the mystery hunters," Barry smiled.

"Just because we found out who was stealing things out of the lockers," grunted Tim. "That wasn't such a big job."

"Anybody could have done it, if he had taken the trouble to," Kent said.

"The biggest surprise about the whole thing was the fact that a boy like Carter Wolf was doing it," Mac put in.

Proceeding slowly along the sidewalk toward home, the four boys once more discussed the recent events which had resulted in earning the name of "mystery hunters." For a long time someone had been stealing athletic supplies and even rings and watches from the gymnasium locker room. Persistent efforts had been made to trap the thief, but without success. Finally the four boys had entered the case, chiefly because a birthday ring of Mac's had been among the things taken. But for a long time they had not made any progress. The prowler seemed to know exactly what they were about. They even tried sleeping in the locker room, but even this produced no results. Finally they decided on strategy and rigged up a camera. This was placed in another room, at a place in the wall where a single brick had been knocked out. The locker doors were hooked up in such a way that when one of them was opened, the camera would operate.

They got immediate results with this. And on the day they took the camera down, a certain wealthy boy named Carter Wolf left school. The negative, when developed, showed that Carter Wolf was the guilty one. His startled face was turned toward the camera, whose click he had heard, and one hand was plainly seen opening a locker door. At first he denied the charges, but finally he had made good the losses in one way or another. Mac was lucky enough to get his ring back, but others found that their property had been sold to pay gambling debts that Wolf had contracted. Only the influence and pleading of his father had saved the boy from the punishment he richly deserved. For the time being he had disappeared from the community, but not until he had left a threat behind him.

"I'll even scores with that Barry Garrison bunch," he had promised.

With the identification of the mysterious sneak thief a wave of relief had swept over Cloverfield High School. The teachers and students were grateful to the four boys whose persistence had finally caught the prowler. The good-natured title of "mystery hunters" had been given them, and the boys knew that under it lay a genuine admiration for the piece of work that they had done.

"When you figure it all out," Kent declared, as they stopped a moment before the brownstone house in which Barry lived, "there wasn't much to it. Maybe there would be a different story if we ever ran up against a real mystery."

"Mysteries are few and far between," Tim said. "Let's talk about something more vital. We'll have about ten days of vacation at Christmas time. What'll we do with it?"

"Eat popcorn and candy off the Christmas tree," Mac grinned.

"Our tree won't have enough on to keep us eating very long," Tim answered. "Shall we do a little winter camping?"

"Either that or hunt some," Barry agreed. "Let's give it some thought in the next few days."

The other boys went on down the street, while Barry turned in at the door of the brownstone house. Kent lived two doors beyond, and the twins lived around the corner in a big frame house. The Fords were not among the wealthiest people in the town, although Mr. Ford did have a fairly good business in dry goods. But they were a fine family, and Kent and Barry had been fond of the two lively boys since grammar-school days.

As Barry entered the hall, his sister Pearl was going up the stairs. In the library to the right of him he could see his father, seated under a lamp, reading a magazine. The rattling of a pan on the stove told him where his mother was.

Pearl was in her first year of high school and had preceded him home by several minutes. She paused a moment on the upper landing to address him.

"Here is the chief of the mystery hunters!" she called cheerfully. "Do you know that everybody is calling you that?"

"Yes, I know it," he nodded. "I wish they would forget it."

Mr. Garrison looked up from his magazine. "I need some real mystery hunters right now," he said. "If you want to take on a real puzzler, come ahead."

Barry was at once interested. His father was a lawyer and frequently handled important cases. The boy placed his books on a hall table and walked into the library.

"What's it all about, Dad? What mystery are you talking about?"

Mr. Garrison took off his glasses and wiped his eyes. "I was thinking about that haunted hunting lodge up on Lake Arrowtip," he said. "But I was only joking when I told you to come ahead. It is a job that will test the brains of an expert detective."

CHAPTER II
The Story of the Haunted Lodge

Barry sat down in one of the big chairs and faced his father. Mr. Garrison had put his magazine aside and was looking thoughtfully at his son.

"A haunted lodge, Dad? Where is it? What haunts it?"

The lawyer laughed. "One question at a time, son! I knew that you would want to know about it as soon as I mentioned that it was haunted, or supposed to be haunted. Because of course it isn't."

"Then what makes people say that it is? Tell me something about it, Dad. Where is it located on Lake Arrowtip?"

"Right about the middle of the lake, on a high bluff that commands a magnificent view up and down the big sheet of water. It is the hunting lodge that belongs to Mrs. Morganson, one of my clients. Some years ago she had that fine big lodge built and used to go up there once in a while herself, though she hasn't been there in late years. You know Lake Arrowtip fairly well, don't you?"

"Yes, I've hiked and camped up there with Kent and the twins. I think I know where that lodge is. Isn't it a big log house with a porch looking out over the lake, off in the direction of Rake Island?"

"Yes, that is the place. Ever been in it?"

"No, but we've passed it in a canoe. There was a party at the lodge at the time. There is another cabin close by, a small log building."

"Yes, that is the Bronson cabin. It is owned by a retired lawyer friend of mine, and he never uses it any more. It is very close to the lodge."

"Well, tell me about this mystery, Dad. Do the people around there think the place is haunted?"

"There aren't very many people around there to think that, but some of our town people won't go to the place. I suppose you remember that Mrs. Morganson's nephew disappeared up there over a year ago and has never been found."

Barry slung one leg over the arm of the chair. "I do remember hearing something about that," he replied. "Wasn't he kidnaped and carried off to Canada somewhere?"

11

"It seemed so," his father nodded. "There was one letter from Canada, telling his aunt not to worry, that he was being well treated. But no trace of him has ever been discovered, and some splendid detectives have been looking for Felix Morganson. Well, since the time that he disappeared, things haven't been going well at Bluff Lodge."

"Is that when the haunting began?" Barry asked.

"A little later than that. You see, Felix Morganson disappeared during a Thanksgiving party at the lodge. There was quite a crowd at the lodge, and they were enjoying a gathering at the time. Along about ten o'clock or so at night Mr. Morganson walked out of the place smoking a cigarette. Several saw him go, but no one asked him where or why he was going. As time went on they missed him, and finally some of the men walked out on the bluff which overlooks the lake, following his footsteps in the light snow that had fallen. Close to the edge of the bluff they found the snow kicked and scuffed up and his cigarette only partially smoked. Then there were long, dragging marks in the snow that seemed to indicate that he had been pulled along down the path to the lake. All trace of him was lost at that point, because the lake was frozen over and the ice was as smooth as glass."

Barry was absorbed in the story. "No one in the lodge heard anything? No outcry or anything?"

His father shook his head. "No. But that same night a servant, a Frenchman, disappeared. He was a man that had been hired to cook and to wait on the tables, and this man was gone. No one knows whether he had anything to do with it all or not, but he left the lodge about the same time Felix Morganson did. No trace of him was ever found."

"How long after the disappearance of Mr. Morganson before they heard from him?"

"About a month later. Then a hastily scrawled letter came from a little town in Canada, telling his aunt that he was well and not to worry. He stated that he did not have time to write any more at the moment. Of course the detectives hustled up to that town, but so far have been unable to learn anything or to uncover a single clue."

"He has been missing well over a year now, hasn't he?" Barry mused.

"Yes, because Thanksgiving was three weeks ago, and it was at that time that he vanished. The queer part about it all is the fact that no request for a ransom was ever received. Mrs. Morganson is quite wealthy, and a considerable sum could be raised among the friends of Felix. But there has never been any demand."

"It's funny." Barry slumped lower in the chair, his mind busy with the details of the event. "But how about this haunting that you spoke of? That came later, didn't it?"

"About three months after Felix Morganson disappeared," Mr. Garrison answered. "Besides going up there herself once in a while, Mrs. Morganson also rents the place out to sportsmen who go up for the winter season to hunt, and to those that go there in the summer to fish. Well, late in January a group of sportsmen went there, and the understanding was that they would stay about three weeks. But at the end of one week they gave it up and took a smaller place down at the tip of the lake. They complained of ghostly rappings, or knocks on the door and no one there when they opened, and they also complained that some of their things had been stolen."

"Sounds foolish," Barry said.

"We thought it was, at first. You see, I handle all of Mrs. Morganson's business, and I had rented the place to these men, who came from Connecticut. We thought for a while that they were just cranky and let it go at that. But two weeks later another party went in, and it was the same thing over again. Added to that, one of the men had an expensive fur coat stolen, and he wanted to bring suit against us. It seems that they heard about the experience of the former party and claimed that we had rented the lodge to them under false pretenses. We had some trouble getting out of that."

"It must be just some ordinary thief that lives in the woods near there," Barry ventured.

"If so, he goes around annoying everybody that puts up in the lodge. Later in the year some fishermen took over the place, and they had similar experiences, and, besides all that, they found their fishing boat scuttled one morning, three holes bored in it. Fortunately we had told them the reputation that the place was getting, but they had just laughed at it. They came away mad as hornets. Well, you can see what it is all doing. No one will rent the lodge now, and it had a long list of prospective renters once. The value of it keeps going down, and since we cannot rent or sell it at a decent price, it is standing idle."

"Does Mrs. Morganson want to sell it?"

"She does now. We have both become so tired of the place and its problem that we would like nothing better than to get it off our hands. There is only one buyer at present, a man named Brand Curry, but he wants it at a price so low that we won't even discuss it. The man never comes to me, he always goes directly to Mrs. Morganson."

"But look here, Dad, did you ever have a detective on the case? Ever have any one go up there?"

"Oh, yes. I have had two private investigators spend some time on the case. One of them didn't find anything or have any kind of an experience. But the other man did. He was a big, chunky fellow named Riley, and he said he could catch anything he went after. Said he would come home dragging the ghost or spook, or whatever it was, by the neck. He remained there two days and then came back and resigned from the case. The first night he was kept busy investigating thumps all over the place, and the second night his shoes and shirt were mysteriously whisked away somehow and he was in a fix because he hadn't taken any baggage with him. He had to go to Fox Point and outfit himself there, and he had to go down there without shirt or shoes. He didn't hear anything that night, and all the time he was there he didn't see anything. He was a disgusted man when he came back here, and it was his opinion that the National Guard should be ordered up there."

Barry and his father laughed at the plight of the private detective who had been so sure of victory over the haunting presence at Bluff Lodge. "But of course, Dad, you believe that someone is doing all this for a purpose?"

"I can't see any other explanation," his father confessed. "But I can't figure out any reason for it. Why should anyone want to frighten

14

camping parties that way? And who is clever enough to make raps and groans and knocks and yet disappear before anyone can spot him? That lodge stands pretty well out of the trees, and no one could dodge behind some convenient tree trunk after every one of these meaningless pranks. As for the disappearance of Mr. Riley's shirt and shoes, that isn't so much of a mystery, after all. The window was open in his room, and anyone could have fished the clothing out. He is lucky that they didn't steal anything more and put him in a bad position."

"That is one thing that convinces me that the spook is a clever one," Barry said. "An amateur or a plain fun maker would have stolen all of his things. This one took just enough to create an air of mystery."

The kindly face of Mrs. Garrison appeared in the doorway. "Supper is ready," she smiled. Barry and his father walked out of the room together.

"Dad," said Barry, "that's a real mystery. I'd like nothing better than to go up there with some of the boys and nose around a bit. Maybe we could find out something."

His father smiled and slapped him on the back. "Aren't you taking that title of 'mystery hunter' a little seriously, Barry?"

"Maybe I am, Dad, but you never can tell. I still think our bunch could find out something of value. Just try us and see."

CHAPTER III
Planning an Expedition

Shortly after supper Barry Garrison left the house and crossed the grass in the direction of Kent's home. But he was saved the trouble of a journey to his chum's house by the appearance of Kent himself. He came dashing down the walk and joined Barry.

"Going for a walk?" he hailed.

"I'm going down to Sadler's store and get my ice skates," Barry replied. "I left them there to be sharpened. Thought you'd like to go along."

"Glad to," nodded Kent, falling into step beside him. "I want to do some studying a little later, and, after the supper I ate, I felt the need for a brisk walk. I was going to drop in and see you for a second before going back to the midnight oil."

"I wanted to see you," Barry informed him. "I've got quite an idea in my head for our winter vacation."

"What? A hunting trip?"

"Yes, but not hunting animals. Hunting spooks!"

"What?" Kent demanded. "What did you say?"

"I said hunting spooks. Or ghosts or haunts or something. Think we could take a photograph of a rapping spook?"

"I don't know what you're talking about," Kent growled. "It all sounds goofy to me!"

Barry laughed. "It did to me, when my father was telling me about it. Tune in to the proper station while I tell you something about it."

"I'm tuned in," Kent said. "You'll have to make it a good one, or it will all be static. Let's hear it."

As the two of them walked slowly toward the business section of Cloverfield, Barry related the story which he had heard from his father. Kent's light and scornful attitude vanished as he listened, and he soon became as deeply interested as Barry had been. Their steps became slower, and they no longer felt the coldness of the night air. They had arrived outside the brightly lighted window of the hardware store just as Barry finished, and they lingered a moment to discuss it.

"That's a first-class mystery," Kent declared. "I'd like to go up there and snoop around some."

"That's just what I had in mind," Barry told him. "I talked about it with Dad at the supper table, and he wasn't very keen about it at first, but finally he said it wouldn't hurt anything for us to go up there and look around. He said he would try and get permission for us to camp in the Bronson cabin, which is in sight of the lodge. How does that strike you?"

"Right on the bull's-eye," answered Kent, promptly. "We can hike up there in two days."

"We can skate up there in less time than that," Barry said. "The Buffalo River runs into the lake about two miles below the cabin and the lodge, and we could go that way. Even if we don't accomplish a thing toward solving the mystery, we will at least have a good vacation, taking in a skating trip and camping in a cabin."

"Sure thing! We've never camped in a cabin. Say, look who is in the hardware store."

Following the direction of Kent's nod, Barry glanced through the glass, and his eyes rested on the form of a boy about their own age, who was examining a sleeping bag. This young man was well dressed and wore an expensive fur coat. On a counter near by a pile of camping equipment lay spread out. Barry recognized the boy at once. It was Carter Wolf, the one who had been detected stealing from the lockers at school.

"Looks like Wolf is going somewhere," he said.

"Going to have a lot of duffle with him, too," added Kent. "This is the first time we've seen him since our affair of the locker room. Let's see if he greets us with politeness."

They entered the store. There was only one clerk in attendance, and he was busy with Carter Wolf. Just as they closed the door they heard Wolf purchase the sleeping bag. He saw the boys and flushed slightly, but contented himself with merely turning his back on them.

"Anything else, Mr. Wolf?" the clerk asked. Wolf consulted a list which he held in his hand.

"Just one thing more," he answered. "I want a lantern."

The clerk quickly procured one from stock. "You're buying a lot of stuff, Mr. Wolf," he smiled. "Must be going on a camping trip somewhere."

Wolf raised his voice slightly. "I am. A bunch of us are going up to camp on Lake Arrowtip."

Barry and Kent exchanged glances and then looked frankly at the goods which Wolf had purchased. They were expensive things, and there was no doubt that the rich boy was planning a real winter camping trip. Fishing tackle and an ax for ice fishing, an old stove, a rifle and several boxes of shotgun shells, a hunting coat and cap, two pairs of boots, the sleeping bags for two other members of his party, and a handsome hunting knife. He gave directions for having the goods sent to his home and then left the store, ignoring the presence of the boys.

"Wonder whom he is going camping with?" Kent asked, as they waited for the ice skates to be wrapped up.

"He goes with a crowd of fellows from Harrison," Barry said. "Probably they are the ones who will go. He evidently intends to be right in our territory, so we'll have to make room for one another. I don't like him well enough to want to be very near him or his crowd."

"I don't, either," Kent agreed. "He could be a nice fellow if he tried hard, but it is easier to be the other way. Trouble with him is, his daddy has always spoiled him. Well, we'll be in a cabin, so we'll probably not conflict with one another."

They left the store and walked toward home, still discussing the thing nearest their minds. Close to Barry's house they met the twins, who were just striding along under a lamplight.

"We'll have some news for them that will open their eyes," Kent chuckled.

The twins bore down on them. "Here you are!" Mac cried. "Tell us all about the trip to Arrowtip Lake!"

"Yes," chimed in Tim. "When do we go up to the haunted lodge and get busy?"

CHAPTER IV
A Strange Conversation

Barry and Kent surveyed the grinning Ford boys for a moment in silence, "the wind taken right out of their sails," as Kent said afterwards. Then Barry grunted.

"Where'd you fellows hear about that lodge?" he demanded.

"That won't be much trouble to answer," Kent declared, before either of the boys could speak.

"They have been to your house, and Pearl told Mac. Whatever you tell one of them, you tell the other."

Mac's only answer to the charge was a bland grin which admitted nothing, but Barry knew that Kent was right. His sister Pearl was an avowed friend of Mac's, and the school chatter always linked their names together.

"I might have known it," Barry said. "Well, as far as that goes, it wasn't any secret from you fellows, but it mustn't get all over town. I'll warn Pearl to keep it quiet. I suppose you'll want to go along."

"Do we!" cried Tim. "Try and leave us home!"

"What do you think about skating up Buffalo River to the lake?" Kent asked.

"Good idea," Mac approved. "There are a couple of places where we'll have to leave the ice and hike."

"I know that," Barry acknowledged. "But we can skate most of the way. How much of the story did Pearl tell you?"

They stood under the street light in a group, and the Ford boys told what they had learned. Pearl knew most of the events that had taken place at Bluff Lodge, and with only a few details Barry completed the story. All the boys were now more eager than ever before to go.

"Let's keep the mystery part a secret," Kent urged. "We'll simply give out the information that we are going on a Christmas-vacation camping trip. That is partly true and is as much as anyone else needs to know."

"Do you think we'll run afoul of Wolf and his bunch?" Tim asked.

21

"I hardly think so," was Barry's reply. "We won't let them worry us if we do see them. Well, I want to get on home and do a little studying. Are you twins through with yours?"

It developed that the twins had simply gone out for a walk after their evening meal and had dropped in first at Kent's and then at Barry's home. It was the custom of the four boys to stroll some after supper and then buckle down to their studies. They all made fair grades in school, and Kent was the outstanding one among them.

"Are you fellows going to win that soccer game against Berkley?" Kent asked the Fords, as they lingered for a moment in front of Barry's door. His question immediately plunged them into a discussion concerning the soccer game, now only two days off. Tim and Mac were on the team, but Kent and Barry had cast in their lots with the gymnasium group.

They finally separated, somewhat reluctant to split up, as they were devoted friends, and the study table was less to be desired than their companionship. But as Mac expressed it, "all good things have to come to an end, even a plate of ice cream!" and with that the soccer players started off on a sprint around the corner, while Barry and Kent went to their front doors with less forceful energy.

Two days later Cloverfield went to Berkley to play soccer. The team had gone down earlier in the day in a big bus, and the rooters followed in cars and on the train. Barry and Kent decided to go by rail, as it was a short trip and not too expensive, so they caught the proper train and were soon in the small town and on their way to the athletic field.

The game was a stirring one, and the two boys in the stand were gripped by it. The two teams battled up and down the field fiercely, driving the ball forward and being hurled back. It became so exciting that Barry and Kent left the stand and followed the teams from one end of the field to the other.

"Too doggone cold to sit in the stand today, anyway," Barry said.

Both teams were battling for a secure position in the school conference, and victory today meant something. The boys who had run out on the field in the short trousers and thin, sleeveless jerseys

22

were now warm and glowing with the swift running and kicking and blocking. It seemed as though it must end in a scoreless tie.

Mac and Tim had been battling to the limit. Tim bore down on a Berkley kicker and leaped into the air, blocking the sailing ball. Racing around the almost spent player, Tim dashed into position to kick the ball across the goal line. But the safety man was facing him, ready to boot the football far down the field and out of danger. Just then Tim saw his brother cut loose and leave the tangled group. Mac's voice reached him in husky pleading.

Tim kicked the ball across on an angle, and Mac's toe met it with a mighty boot that abruptly changed its course. Caught off guard, the goal tender made a mad dive for the oncoming ball. But he was a fraction too late, and the soccer ball flashed across for the first goal and point.

Kent and Barry joined enthusiastically in the wild cheer that went up from Cloverfield rooters. In the next six minutes that remained, Berkley fought fiercely to even the score, but Cloverfield fought as grimly to turn them back and prevent them from scoring. In this they were successful, and the game ended with a victory in favor of the visiting team by the score of one to nothing.

"Great work that the twins did," approved Barry, as they followed the crowd out of the stand section.

"You're right," nodded Kent. "That gives us the edge on the championship. We'll congratulate the boys when we see them at home."

They found quite a crowd assembled at the station, and their train was not due for some time. There was a holiday spirit among the people, and the station was decorated with wreaths and sprigs of Christmas greens. Toys and candy were displayed in one case. The stoves at each end of the station glowed, and the heat felt good.

Kent and Barry joined a group of home school boys and chatted. Presently Barry left the circle and walked over to the counter to buy a newspaper. Obtaining one, he glanced over the headlines and then turned to the sport page. There were some comments on games and players, and he sat down on a high-backed station seat to read. On the other side two men were seated and talking, but Barry was too absorbed even to glance their way. It was a chance phrase that caught his attention.

"Anything new on that Bluff Lodge deal?" a voice asked.

The voice that answered was coarse and husky. "No. The old lady don't want to accept my price. But let her hold out if she wants to. The value don't go up any. Not on that place."

There was a pause. Barry's eyes were still on the print, but he did not see it. His ears were listening keenly. It was possible that they were talking about some other place than the haunted lodge. The words of the first man came to him once more.

"Nobody will rent the place. She'll be ready to give it away before long."

At that moment the train puffed into the station, drowning out every other sound. Barry growled inwardly. "It would have to get in just at this moment!" Folding his paper, he stood up casually and looked after the two men, who were walking out to board the train. One was tall and thin, and the other was short and chunky. He was unable to see the face of either one clearly.

"Now I wonder who those fellows are," he mused. "No doubt Dad will know them, if they are connected in any way with Bluff Lodge. And from the way they talked, they have an interest in that place."

CHAPTER V
The Start Upriver

A few days after the victorious soccer game with Berkley the high school closed for the Christmas vacation. With whoops of joy the boys and girls poured out of the institution of learning and started home, eager for the holiday and all the good things connected with it. A light snow had fallen the night before, and the country was clothed with a blanket of white.

"Tomorrow night Tim will sit up and try to see what Santa Claus looks like," Mac grinned, as the four boys walked down the main street. "He always does, until Pa chases him to bed. He——"

Tim cut his speech short by neatly planting a hastily packed snowball back of Mac's ear. His brother returned the fire, and finally Kent and Barry joined in, the fun becoming fast and furious. A group across the street began to bombard them, and then the four chums turned on the common enemy. In this manner, enjoying the sharp air and the good-natured fun, the boys came to Barry's door and stopped for a final word.

"When shall we get started?" Tim asked.

"I think we ought to light out on the morning after Christmas," Barry said.

"I don't know about that," Kent objected. "We have to buy some provisions and pack our sled, and we won't want to do that on Christmas. Let's make it two days after the great holiday."

The others agreed to this. "As far as I can see, nobody knows why we are going," Mac said.

"No, I think everyone believes that we are just going off on a camping trip," said Barry. "That is what we want them to think. After all, we may not learn a thing about the mystery, and in that case our trip will be just a winter camp."

"But we'll work like the dickens to get a line on the spook," promised Kent, as they parted.

Christmas Day was cold and gray, and late in the afternoon it began to snow. For several hours the light flakes fell, and the boys were beginning to worry. If the snow became too deep, their trip would have to be put off, and it looked very much as though the ice on the river would be covered in such a way that skating would be impossible. But the day following the holiday a wind blew the snow into drifts and banks and Kent reported that the river was clear enough to skate on.

Christmas Day passed off quietly, and the boys enjoyed it. There were gifts and family gatherings and a cheery air in general. The next day they busied themselves, preparing to go on their trip. In Kent's barn there was a wide, low sled, and they began to pack it with supplies and food. Late in the afternoon they stood in a group and surveyed it.

"Guess everything is on there," Barry said thoughtfully.

"I can't think of anything else," Kent admitted.

"Who is going to pull the sled at the start?" Tim asked, roping an ax down firmly.

Kent winked at Barry. "Seems like you twins ought to pull it all the way," he said. "You are both the same size and would show up well in harness!"

"We wouldn't look any better than you would," Mac retorted. "Let's flip a coin to see who pulls first."

Several tosses of the coin indicated that Kent was to pull the sled first, and the twins pounded him on the back in derision. Darkness was now falling fast, and they separated for the night.

"What time are we starting?" Tim asked.

"We'll get going at eight o'clock," Barry decided. "There isn't any great hurry. We'll hunt a little on the way up there and can camp out tomorrow night."

To the four boys, impatient to be on their way, the night seemed a long one, but the day of the start finally came and they were ready to go. Mr. Garrison had a final word with Barry.

"Here are the keys to the Bronson cabin, and this one is for the lodge," he told his son, as the latter laced up his high-top lumberman shoes. "You can look around all you want to, but keep out of trouble. I'd rather that you would not camp in the lodge unless there seems to be some good reason for doing so."

"All right," Barry agreed. "But it will be permissible to look through the place, won't it, Dad?"

"Oh, surely. I want you to go through the lodge, but I think you'll be more comfortable in Bronson's cabin. The lodge is a big, rambling place and not easy to heat. Have a good time, and start back in time for school again."

Barry promised, and after bidding his family good-bye he was off on a trot across the intervening yards to Kent's barn. He found his companions there, tying a few last minute articles fast. They greeted him joyously.

"We were just going over to ask your mother if you were up yet!" Mac hailed.

"She would have told you that I've been up a long time," Barry smiled.

Kent slung his skates over his shoulder. "I guess we're ready to go," he said. "Who'd we decide had to pull the sled?"

"You know who," Tim answered. "It won't be any weight to pull when it gets on the ice."

The mystery hunters set off for the Buffalo River, which flowed close to the residential section of Cloverfield. It was a clear, cold day, and their spirits rose with each step forward. The sun sparkled on the snowbanks and the icicles, until all the landscape flashed with beauty. All four of them rejoiced to be alive and able to go.

"I just feel like I could strike out and skate for hours," Mac said.

"It's a dandy day for a snow fight like we had at the high school last year," Kent observed. "In fact, a fellow would feel like doing about anything on a day like this."

"Except being at home with the mumps or something," Tim chuckled.

"There is the old river," Barry said, as they came in sight of the Buffalo. "Now we can get into real action."

They sat on a rotted log beside the river and put on their skates. It was a cold job, and more than once they paused to blow on chilled fingers. But at last the skates were adjusted and the campers were ready to swing up the river toward Lake Arrowtip. They clumped

27

down the side of the bank and slid out on the ice, cutting a few circles by way of warming up. Kent hooked the rope of the sled to the belt of his Mackinaw.

"I guess we're about ready," he nodded, and with a ringing sound the runners of the skates slid forward and they were away on their journey upriver.

For over a mile they kept up a fast pace and then moderated it somewhat, settling down to an even gait that would take them a long way from home if maintained for any length of time. They passed a few skaters and one group of high school boys in particular, with whom they paused to chat. From them they gleaned the information that Carter Wolf and some of his friends had started on their trip, going in a roundabout way by motor truck.

"They'll find it a rough journey over any of these roads to Lake Arrowtip," Barry commented, as they resumed their skating.

"I'd rather go this way or even to hike it," Kent nodded.

"I guess Wolf would rather go the most comfortable way," Mac observed. "I'll bet the truck was heated in some way. I'm even surprised that Wolf will go camping in the winter time."

Leaving Cloverfield far behind them, the boys followed the little river into the deep woods. In the forest the stream became narrower, but there was room for all of them, and they had gone seven miles before it became necessary to leave the ice sheet and take to the shore. They came at last to a place where a log was frozen broadside into the ice and a mass of refuse spoiled the smooth, glassy surface.

"First detour," sang out Barry. "What do you say we hike some and see if we can bring down a rabbit?"

The others were agreeable, and they took to the shore. The trees were sufficiently far back from the banks to allow them to proceed. Pulling the sled was harder, and Barry relieved Kent of it. They tramped along, and just before noon Mac took a shot at a squirrel, but missed.

"Bum shot," he exclaimed, in disgust.

"You needn't lament over that," Kent consoled. "It would be quite a job to bring that lightning dodger down with a rifle."

At noontime they halted and made temporary camp. The twins cut into the wet wood and hewed to the center for the dry heart of it. The other two boys scraped away the snow and piled some rocks for a fireplace. After some fanning and blowing, the damp wood caught fire and blazed up.

Kent searched among the articles on the sled and then straightened up. "Say, look here. Did anybody think to bring coffee?"

The other three boys looked at one another blankly. "I didn't," Barry admitted, and the twins admitted the same.

"We can live without it," Mac pointed out.

"Sure we can, but you know how good it tastes on a camping trip, especially in winter. We haven't even got cocoa along. And I was sure that the sled was fully packed! Is there any place that we can get it along the line?"

"We could swing away from the river a little bit and get it at Fox Point," Barry said.

"We'll do that, then. I guess we can go without it for a few days. Come on and get your plates out."

The journey was resumed immediately after dinner, and they skated for a few miles. Then some rocks made it necessary for them to go around, and they walked some more. Chancing to see an old mill on a branch of the river, they explored it, and before long nightfall was upon them and they stopped to make an overnight camp. Two small camping tents were set up and sleeping bags spread out. Then they made a fireplace and gathered a supply of wood. By the time that the fire was going it was pitch dark, and the flames flashed up into the inky blackness like living tongues, throwing the black tree trunks into bold relief against the white background of the snow-covered earth.

"Fellows, this is just right!" Tim exclaimed, looking around him with delight. Barry and Kent were bent over the fire, and Mac was coming in with a load of wood on his shoulder.

"It's colder camping than we are used to," Kent remarked.

Mac threw his load of wood on the ground. "Boys, we may be able to get some coffee," he said. "There is another campfire just a short distance over there."

The others looked up with interest. "Where?" Barry and Kent asked in chorus.

Mac pointed in the direction from which he had brought the wood. "Just a little way over there. I was chopping wood on the top of a knoll, and I could see their fire through the trees."

"We could go over there and borrow some coffee," Tim said.

"It would be nice to know who our neighbors are," Barry commented.

"Unless," said Kent, slowly, "those neighbors happen to be Carter Wolf and his particular friends. If so, the less they know about our whereabouts, the better for us."

CHAPTER VI
Strange Treatment

There was a moment of silence after Kent had spoken. The boys were not afraid of the Wolf boy and his companions, but they had no desire to camp too close to them. Carter possessed a mean spirit, and they felt it best to avoid him wherever possible.

"I hardly believe that they will camp out in the woods," Tim said. "I'll bet they will go to a cabin or some more comfortable place. If it is Wolf, he won't give us any coffee."

"Or sell us any, either," Mac added.

"We wouldn't need to walk right into that other camp," Barry advised. "It ought to be easy to approach the place without making any noise. I think we should find out who is camping there."

"Tim and I will go over and scout around," Mac offered.

"All right," Barry nodded. "We'll get supper ready. If anything goes wrong, just sing out and we'll come hopping over."

"Nothing will happen if we get running first," Tim grinned. "Shall we offer to pay for the coffee?"

"Sure," nodded Kent. "They may have a small supply, and we wouldn't want to take it away from them. If they give it to you, that will be all right, but we should offer to buy it."

Tim pushed his camping ax down into his belt case. "Come on, Mac. Let's see where you spotted that fire."

Leaving Barry and Kent at the campfire, the two brothers hiked off into the woods to the knoll where Mac had been cutting wood. It was an uphill climb, and their breath showed in little, frosty clouds before they got to the place. Finally Mac pointed off through the spruce trees.

"There it is. See that fire down there?"

Following the direction of Mac's mittened finger, Tim saw a small point of light down in a hollow. It came evidently from a small fire and appeared to be less than a half-mile away. They were unable to see anything else except the little flame.

"Somebody down there, all right," Tim nodded. "Well, let's go calling."

"And we'll look before we knock," Mac chuckled. "It might be the wrong house!"

They descended the other side of the knoll and tramped on toward the lone campfire. Underfoot the snow crunched and broke with a cold, snapping sound and the rocks were slippery. The stars stood out brilliantly overhead, and they had no difficulty in making their way through the Vermont forest. They rounded a ragged bluff of rock, and the fire was now very near.

"Slow up now and let's get a good look at this outfit," Mac whispered.

Tim nodded silently, and they began to approach the camp as noiselessly as possible. Keeping behind friendly trees, they slipped closer and closer until they could see around the clear space in the center of which a small fire burned fitfully.

"It isn't Wolf and his bunch," Mac whispered.

"No, only a man and a woman," Tim returned, in an equally low tone.

The camp was occupied by a man and a woman. Close beside the fire could be seen some camping equipment, a frying pan which had apparently been placed in the snow while hot, a knapsack, and a brightly colored blanket and a pair of gloves. Against a near-by stump leaned a rifle, and the man had a hunting knife at his belt. They had just finished supper, and the smell of fish lingered on the air. The woman was placing chunks of snow in a pan, and when this was finished she put the pan on the fire. There was a sizzling sound as the snow on the outside of the pot slid into the fire.

Before advancing any further, the boys studied the man and woman closely. They were dark-skinned and looked to be French. Both of them were warmly dressed for winter travel, and their camping equipment was battered and blackened, indicating much use. The woman wore a coat with a rich fur collar, and both of them seemed perfectly at home in the woods. They exchanged no words and were engrossed in their tasks. The man was cleaning scraps from a plate while the woman waited for the snow to melt.

Tim reached over and pushed Mac. "Might as well go to it," he said, and the brothers left the shelter of the trees and approached the camp.

They had advanced several steps before the campers heard them coming. They had left the trees and were crossing the clearing. The woman was the first to hear them, and she lifted her head with a swift motion, and her black eyes seemed to glitter like those of an animal who was trapped. She spoke sharply in French to her companion, who dropped a plate and rose to his feet, his hand running backward toward his hunting knife. The woman looked around at the rifle.

"Hi!" greeted Mac, not very well impressed with the manner of the two campers. "May we come into your camp?"

"Look like you in ze camp now," said the man, without a smile. "What you want?"

"We're camping just over the hill," Mac explained, his eyes on the woman, who had picked up the rifle. She was holding it muzzle down in the crook of her arm, but her eyes stared at them in a way that neither of the boys relished. "We found that we had forgotten to bring any coffee with us, so we saw your fire and came to ask if you could sell us any."

"Sorry if we startled you," Tim added.

"What you want?" the man asked again. The boys looked at him with some astonishment.

"I just told you," Mac answered. "We came to buy some coffee."

"You not come to buy coffee," the man said, his chin coming forward in a way that was far from comforting. "You want somet'ing else, eh? You follow us, eh?"

"We did not," Tim denied, indignantly. "We're camping up here and we saw your fire, that is all."

The woman spoke to her companion. "Pierre, listen!" She launched into rapid French, and when she had finished he shrugged his shoulders. She turned to the boys suddenly. "We not got coffee. We not got anyt'ing. You go back to your camp. Go back!"

She made a quick motion with the rifle, though she did not lift the muzzle, which still pointed downward. There was no mistaking the implied threat or the fact that the boys were not wanted. Mac felt angry at their unfriendly reception, but he felt it best to retreat at once.

"All right," he said. "We only wanted to buy a little coffee. We weren't going to ask you to give it to us. Come along, Tim."

"We got no coffee. We got not'ing," the woman repeated, and the twins turned and walked off, their eyes on the alert for any sudden move. But the woodsman and his wife stood by the flickering fire motionless.

No word was spoken until they were around the rock bluff, and then the boys looked at each other. "What do you make of that?" Tim asked.

"Well, I'll be hanged if I know," Mac cried. "Wasn't that the limit? They acted as if we were a couple of criminals."

"That's probably what they are," Tim advanced. Mac came to a halt.

"Why, of course! He said something about following them. I'll bet those two are a couple of bad eggs. Maybe we're lucky we got away from them."

Tim urged him on. "Let's get back to the camp," he said, looking over his shoulder. "See what the other boys think about it."

When they stalked into camp a delightful smell of pork and beans greeted them. Kent was piling fresh wood on the fire, and Barry was stirring a fork around among the beans. The sled had been cleaned off and was ready to serve as a table.

"Hello, what luck?" Barry hailed. "Get any coffee?"

"All we got was an order to get out of the camp pronto," Mac answered.

"Almost got ordered off with a rifle," Tim added, stooping down and warming his hands over the cook fire.

"What's that?" Barry asked, sharply.

"Was it Wolf's camp?" Kent inquired.

"No, it wasn't. This is what happened." Mac related the story, and the other two boys listened with interest and astonishment.

"Well, you certainly got a cool reception," was Kent's comment.

"Cool!" exploded Tim. "It almost froze us!"

Barry gazed off in the timber in the direction of the hostile camp. "That's a mighty queer way for anyone to act when you just go and ask them to sell you coffee."

"Yes, and they had coffee, too," Mac avowed. "I saw the jar of it. Did you, Tim?"

His brother nodded. "As plain as day, right there beside the fire. But they acted as though we were poison."

They were still discussing it when they sat down to eat, and it furnished the main topic until bedtime. Gradually they drifted to other things and forgot the incident. They did not stay up long after supper. The cold was severe and did not encourage sitting around for more than an hour after the meal. After cutting a big supply of firewood they decided to turn in.

"The good old sleeping bags will serve us well tonight," Kent said, as they prepared to turn in.

Barry brought a pan of melted snow from the fire. "Here is warm water to wash in," he announced. "Hurry up and get at it, or it will freeze."

Tim was the first one to wash, and he toweled his face and neck with chattering teeth. "Good night, but this is cold business," he ejaculated. "Too icy to wash behind the ears tonight."

Mac pulled off his shoes and shirt and sat on the sleeping bag while he washed. Then with a yell he slipped inside the warm lining of the bag, doubling up. "Boy, doesn't this feel good!"

It did not take the others long to get into their bags. Barry and Kent shared one tent, and the twins had the other. After a few words they went to sleep, and utter stillness settled over the winter camp.

Several hours later Barry awoke and crawled out of the bag, shivering in the cold air. The fire was low, and he wanted to keep it going so that they could make a quick blaze in the morning. He pulled on his shoes and slipped into his Mackinaw. His hat followed, and then he stepped up and out of the tent, rubbing his hands.

He halted with a little shock. A short man in corduroy trousers and woodsman's boots stood at the edge of the clearing, looking around the camp. At sight of Barry he crouched and fairly sprang into the bushes, beating a retreat from the place. His form had been shadowy and indistinct. Barry roused from his state of surprise.

"Here!" he called out, sharply. "What do you want? Who are you?"

There was no answer from the one who had been watching the camp. All was profoundly silent.

CHAPTER VII
At Bronson's Cabin

Kent stirred and sat up in his sleeping bag. In the dimness of the tent he saw that Barry was not there. He heard the twins move and say something in the next tent. Then Kent seemed to remember that someone had spoken.

"Where are you, Barry?"

"Out here," came the answer. "Somebody has been in the camp."

Kent and the twins joined him as soon as possible. Barry was heaping more wood on the fire.

"You say somebody was in the camp?" Kent asked.

Barry pointed to the spot where the man had stood. "A man was standing there when I just came out to put more wood on the fire. I couldn't make his face out very well, but he was a short, stocky fellow, and I just took it that he was the Frenchman you boys saw."

"I'll bet it was," Tim answered. "Any of our things missing?"

Barry shook his head. "I believe not—at least I can't see that anything is. It looked to me as if he had just arrived. What time is it, anyway?"

Mac tugged his watch out of his pocket and looked at the dial by the light of the fire. "Ten minutes past three a. m.," he announced.

"I suppose they have broken camp and are on their way," said Tim. "They may have just stopped by to take a look at us. You didn't see the woman?"

"No, and I can't even be sure that the man was that Frenchman. Did he have on brown corduroy pants and a checked Mackinaw?"

"Yes," the twins nodded.

"Then that's who it was. I could see that much by the feeble light of the fire, though I couldn't see his face. Think we ought to go back to bed?"

"I'm too sleepy to sit up for any Frenchman," Kent yawned.

"I don't believe that he'll come back," Mac said. "I'm freezing around here, so I'm on my way back to the bed. Call me for breakfast!"

"Call you nothing!" cried Kent. "Barry and I cooked supper, so you fellows are billed to provide the breakfast."

The others went back to their sleeping bags, and Barry built the fire up before seeking his. When he did crawl back into the soft, warm interior of the bag he did not go to sleep at once. For a long time he lay listening, but no sound broke the stillness, and at last he dozed off and slept soundly. He was awakened by Kent stirring around and crawling over him.

"Let's go see what these twins have for us," his companion invited, and Barry followed as quickly as he could get dressed. The Ford brothers were already on the job, and bacon was curling in the pan. The day was gray and overcast, and it looked as though it might snow.

"I guess our French friend didn't come back," Mac said, forking out bacon on the tin plates. "Everything is about ready to eat. Come and get it."

Breakfast was soon dispatched, and then they put the camp in order. Before long they were on the river again, skating along rapidly, in order to warm up. They had gone scarcely a mile when bodies were warm and blood tingling.

"I hope it doesn't snow until we get to the cabin," Kent said.

"So do I," Barry agreed. "A big fall would work against us."

They had planned to eat one more outdoor meal, but they arrived close to Fox Point around the noon hour, so they had dinner in the country store there, eating sandwiches and drinking hot cocoa at a little table close to the round iron stove that threw out a splendid heat. They bought the coffee that they lacked and then started once more. At last they skated out on the broad expanse of ice that marked Lake Arrowtip.

"Here we are at last," Mac whooped. "Let's have a race down the lake to the cabin."

"You can't do it," Barry objected. "See how that snow is spread out? You go a little way and then you have to walk across a snow bar and strike the ice on the other side. You just can't keep going."

"That's all the better," spoke up Kent. "It will be an obstacle race. Skate on the ice, run across the snow, and skate some more. Let's line up and go!"

38

"I'm pulling the sled," Barry reminded them. "But you fellows go to it and I'll follow on. Are you ready? Get set. Go!"

The three racers were off like a shot, striking out across the clear ice of Lake Arrowtip. Coming to the soft snow that spread across their path, they leaped into it and ran through as fast as their skates would allow them to. Again they were out on clear ice, and for a time they skated furiously, with Mac slightly in the lead. Then another and longer island of snow slowed them down, and Tim tipped over, tumbling in the path of Kent, who had to swerve to avoid going down. By the time that Kent got on the ice again, Mac was far ahead and turned around in a swift circle and gave the race up, waiting for the others to catch up with him.

Barry skated on in a more leisurely manner, drawing the sled after him and taking in the beauty of Lake Arrowtip. He had visited the place in the spring and summer, but had never seen it in the grip of the New England winter. It presented now the picture of a broad flooring of ice, with the dark lines of pine and hemlock ringing it around. From the lake the hills ran up sharply, flowing into the mountains, blanketed with a thick white carpet of snow. Out in the middle of the lake stood Rake Island, a rugged little thumb of land covered with brush and timber and rough rocks.

Behind them the lake was broad, but before them it narrowed. Barry could now see the Bronson cabin and beyond it the roof of the lodge. His heart beat faster, and unconsciously he skated on with increased speed. They were close to the scene of the mysterious events that had interested him so much.

He joined the others, and they were soon at the bank before the Bronson cabin. Taking off their skates, they walked up the slope to this plain little log house, but their eyes were on the big hunting lodge. It stood on a bluff and could be approached only in a roundabout way from the lake, up the sides of the slopes and not from the front.

"There it is, the house of mystery," cried Tim, as they took in the length of the low log lodge building.

"It looks cold and deserted," Mac offered. "Doesn't look as though it has any spooks around it at this time of year. Bet you a doughnut we don't learn a thing."

"That's a mighty poor spirit to start our hunt with," Barry objected, as he felt in his pocket for the key to the Bronson cabin.

Up to the moment they had paid no attention to the cabin in which they were going to live, but now, as Barry unlocked the door, they scanned it with interest. It was nearly square and was made of rough hewed logs. It appeared to be very old, and there was only one small window to the left of the door. A rock chimney pushed its way through the roof.

"We'll like this place when we get used to it," Kent predicted.

Barry pushed the door open, and they entered. There was a large general room, and a small lean-to which served as a kitchen. A single bed with sooty covers was pushed up against the wall on one side of the room. A wide fireplace with rusty andirons in it showed at the back of the cabin room. Everything was dirty and dreary-looking.

"Hasn't been used for some time," Tim commented, as they stood and looked around.

"No," Barry admitted. "Dad said it hadn't. We'll have a lot of cleaning and fixing to do. Also, we'll have to sleep on the floor in our sleeping bags, as there is only one bed in the place, and it doesn't look very inviting. Well, how about it? Shall we go to work?"

The others were entirely agreeable, and they set to with a will. There was an abundance of work for everyone, and so the afternoon hours sped away. Just before dark they united their efforts and cut enough wood for the winter evening. It was dark when they had gathered enough, and then they turned their attention to supper. There was a rusty iron stove in the lean-to, and between that and the open fireplace they managed without any trouble. Supper was a happy affair, and when the wind rose a little later, they congratulated themselves that they had a warm cabin to camp in.

"And it looks a heap cleaner than it did when we came here," Mac remarked, looking around with satisfaction.

40

They spent the long evening chatting around the fireplace and at last sought their sleeping bags on the log floor before the fire. Barry opened the door to throw out some wash water and stood for a moment, his eyes fixed on the darker mass of the lodge building.

"Tomorrow we'll look into that place," he reflected. "I wonder what the secret of it is, anyway? Well, I hope we'll be lucky enough to find out. Maybe the haunt will be around tonight to look us over!"

CHAPTER VIII
The Upstairs Window

The boys slept soundly throughout the night, and it was seven o'clock before Tim opened his eyes and looked around the unfamiliar interior of the Bronson cabin. For a moment he was unable to place himself, and then the events of the previous evening came to him. A glance at his companions showed that they were still asleep. The fire had long since gone out, and the place was cold. He struggled up into a sitting position.

"It certainly is cold in here," he decided, slipping out of the warm bag. "I'll get our fire going at once. And believe me, I want a more comfortable bed than that one was!"

He shivered while pulling on his clothes, and it was with satisfaction that he drew his heavy sweater down over his head. Then he looked around for water in which to wash, but the little that they had was frozen.

"No bath until after I get the fire under way and melt some snow," he thought. "I'll probably need a wash worse after building the fire than I do now, anyway."

Kent woke up and looked at him sleepily. "Hello, half-size! You're an early bird, I see!"

"Yes, I am, full-size!" Tim retorted, reaching for his ax. "I'm going out and gather worms for the rest of you lazy birds!"

"Fine!" Kent approved. "Hurry up and get a fire going, so that I can get up!"

"Anyone who isn't up by the time I come back with wood will get a snow rub," promised the Ford twin.

All of the wood had been used up on the previous night, and Tim was compelled to go out and hunt for a fresh supply. Accordingly he stepped out onto the hard-packed snow before the cabin, his eyes quickly taking in the lake and the surrounding country. For a moment he paused, taking in the beauty of it all, unconsciously drawing a deep breath of satisfaction.

The sun was rising over the tops of the spruce and hemlocks and striking fire on the sheet of ice. Icicles gleamed from the roof slope of

43

the big hunting lodge. At the edge of the timber a rabbit hopped out into the clearing, looked around with a jerk of his brown head, and then streaked off into the undergrowth.

"By ginger, it's a dandy morning. And those sleepyheads in there!"

Tim knew that it was warm and comfortable in the sleeping bags, but the beauty of the new morning was worth looking at. He started off toward the timber to get his supply of wood, and then noticed a small shack close to the cabin. Investigating this, he was delighted to find a small stack of firewood.

"Good luck! This will save me the trouble of cutting a supply right now."

He slipped the camping ax through his belt and carried a heaping armful of wood into the cabin. By this time all of the boys were awake. Kent was dressing, and Mac and Barry still enjoyed the comfort of the bags.

"I'm glad to see that you fellows have decided to get up at last," Tim greeted them.

"We were afraid to face your wrath if we didn't," Kent smiled. "You got that wood in a mighty big hurry."

"Yes, it was ready-made. Found a small supply of it in a shack around on the other side of the cabin." Tim heaped it into the fireplace and touched a match to the kindling. The boys watched the flame lick upward and then spread with a crackling sound to the remainder of the wood.

"That feels good," Barry approved, getting up. "The whole outfit thanks you, Timmy boy!"

"You can express your gratitude in a more lasting and practical way," Tim informed him. "Now that I have built the fire, suppose you fellows make the breakfast."

"We'll agree to that," Kent said.

Barry began to open the package of bacon. "Tim, as long as you are dressed for the great out-of-doors, suppose you go get that long extension handle for the coffee pot from the sled."

"All right. Where's the sled?"

"Right outside the door," Barry told him.

"I don't remember seeing it there, but I suppose it is," answered Tim, as he made for the door.

Mac rolled up the sleeping bags and put them away. "Do we have to sleep this way every night?" he asked.

"No, we've got to work out some plan for better beds," Barry replied. "This floor is hard and cold."

Tim thrust his head in the doorway. "Say, that sled isn't here!" he called.

"Isn't there?" Kent demanded.

"No, sir, it is not. We left it right here by the door, didn't we?"

Barry hastened to the door, followed by the other boys. "Yes, we left it there, with the long coffee-pot handle and a roll of canvas on top of it." He looked around the ground and off toward the timber. "It is gone, all right. I'd like to know who took it."

Unmindful of the cold, they were all outside, standing in a group around the spot where the sled had been left the night before. The snow was too solidly packed to reveal any marks of the runners.

"Well, that means that somebody was around here last night while we were all sleeping," Barry remarked. "When I threw some water out before I went to bed, I saw the front runner, so the sled was here at that time. Anybody hear anything?"

No one had. As if by common consent they all turned and looked at Bluff Lodge, standing solidly in the rays of the morning sun.

"When are we going to look through that place?" Mac asked.

"Sometime today," Barry promised. "But first we want to see if we can get our sled back." He studied the ground around the front of the cabin. "Not a mark."

"Look here!" cried Tim, who had been doing some hunting on his own account. "Somebody looked in the window at us last night!"

He pointed to a row of fingerprints on the ledge of the window, and the boys crowded around in excitement. There were ten fingermarks in the snow that clung to the outside sill.

"I wonder if those prints were there before we came," Mac mused. "That snow is hard."

45

"They have been made by somebody who leaned down hard," Kent decided, studying the marks. "You can see where the snow broke under his fingers. I didn't look at this window ledge before, so I don't know whether they were here before or not."

None of the boys had noticed the marks, but all of them were inclined to believe that whoever had stolen the sled had peered in the window and had made the prints. They were gripped with a feeling of mystery.

"Things are starting pretty quickly," Barry said, somewhat grimly.

Mac glanced inside the cabin door and then sprinted forward with a shout. "Hey! The coffee is boiling all over the place!"

The accident to the beverage was more of a benefit than an evil, because the boys had been standing in the cold air long enough to feel somewhat chilled. At Mac's frantic whoop they crowded back into the building, and Kent rescued the blackened pot, scorching his hands in the act.

They lost no time now in dispatching breakfast, and during the meal they discussed the trend of events. The fact that someone had been close to them during the night put them on their guard, and they determined to make a search for the missing sled at once.

"We need that sled," Tim declared. "When we go back to town we don't want to have to pack all the stuff on our backs."

"We can do it if we have to," Barry reminded him.

"Of course, but who wants to? I'm wondering if the one or ones who took it did it for a joke or because they needed it."

"Might have been some of Wolf's crowd," Mac suggested.

"We don't even know if they are anywhere near us," Kent protested.

"If they are, I wouldn't put it past them," Mac went on.

They hastily cleaned the dishes and then left the cabin, locking the door after them. Another attempt was made to pick up the trail, but there simply was no track to follow.

"Nothing doing, we'll just have to hike along and see what we can see," Barry decided.

The rest of the morning was spent in a fruitless tramp through the woods. They entered the timber back of the cabin and made a big circle around to the east, going along for several miles until they came out on the ice of the lake. During this time they passed only one home, where they talked for a moment with some poor children, who were the only ones home at the time. In all respects it was a deserted mountain country.

They got back to the cabin at noontime and dragged a dead limb up before the door, planning to chop some firewood a little later. Dinner consisted of a large rabbit that Mac had shot on the morning trip, and after the meal was over the mystery hunters went to work. The twins and Kent began to wash the dishes, and Barry went out to chop the tree that they had dragged in.

The plan for the afternoon was to make another search for the sled, this time on the other side of the hunting lodge. The country in this direction was much wilder than that on the side where the Bronson cabin stood, and just beyond Bluff Lodge they could see the ragged side of an old granite quarry. It was also part of the afternoon program to explore the lodge.

Barry worked on the limb with a sharp, long-handled ax, and soon the pile of stovewood mounted beside him. After a time he paused to rest, leaning on the handle of the ax. The vigorous exercise had made him feel warm. His eyes traveled over to the lodge, and he scanned the place with interest, until one fact struck him forcibly. Quickly he straightened up.

His gaze was fastened upon an upper window in the low loft space of the lodge. This window was partly open, and, as Barry looked, a certain conviction came to him.

"It's a queer thing about that window. I've looked over there several times, and I can positively testify that it wasn't open before!"

47

CHAPTER IX
Inside the Haunted Lodge

Barry lifted the ax and with a single swing of his arm imbedded it in the side of the tree limb. Then he stepped to the door of the cabin and glanced inside. Mac was stacking the dishes up, and the other two boys were just coming out of the lean-to kitchen.

"Come here a minute," Barry called to them. Mac lingered to finish his work.

When they had joined him at the door, he pointed toward the lodge. "See anything strange about the place?" he asked.

Mac joined them in the doorway, and they gazed at the hunting lodge. "Looks the same as ever to me," Tim said.

"No, there is a window half open," Kent cried, pointing.

"That is just what I wanted you to see," Barry told them. "Did any of you notice that it was open before this?"

"I'm sure that it wasn't," Mac said.

"We ought to have seen it before this, if it was," Tim chimed in.

"That is exactly what I thought," Barry replied. "I was cutting wood, and while I was resting, I turned and looked at the place. It came to me at once that all the windows were down the last time we looked that way."

"Then somebody has been in the place while we were off hunting for the sled," Tim observed.

"It looks that way. For some reason he opened that upstairs window and forgot to close it. Fellows, we had better go explore that lodge right now. We can look for the sled later on."

The boys needed no further urging. They were anxious to go through the old place, and now that the window had been opened they were more than eager to enter the lodge. Sweaters and caps were hastily put on, and Barry got the keys to the big building.

"If it hadn't been for looking around for the sled, we would have been in that place this morning," he said.

They crossed the snow to the front porch of Bluff Lodge. This porch extended clear across the log building and gave a magnificent view up and down the lake. Twenty-five yards from the porch the bluff dropped fourteen feet straight down to the waters of Arrowtip.

"Dandy place to sit and look out over the lake on a warm summer day," Kent commented, as Barry fitted his key to the lock.

"It certainly is," his chum agreed. "This lodge ought to be worth quite a bit of money. It would be, too, if it weren't getting a bad name."

By this time Barry had turned the key, and with a grinding sound the bolt shot back. The boys crowded closer to him, anxious for their first glimpse inside the haunted lodge building. Barry swung the door open wide, and they walked in, glancing around with interest.

They found themselves in a wide hall that was square and roomy. A big fireplace took up a wide space on one side of the wall, and over it hung the head of an elk. Pictures adorned the walls, and over a door leading into the other part of the lodge hung an old flintlock gun. A flight of stairs led to the loft.

"This is a dandy place," remarked Mac, as they stood and looked around.

"I wonder if this is the main room, where they sit around the fire?" Kent asked.

Barry moved to the door and pushed it open. "No, this seems to be the living room," he announced, stepping through the doorway. The others followed and found themselves in a big living room, furnished with several chairs and a long couch that was placed in front of the fireplace. Shelves of books and some animal skins were to be seen in this room, and it was unmistakably the guest gathering place.

"This is more like it," Tim remarked, as they explored the room. "That other place is just the front hall. Gosh, but it is cold in here!"

Beside the fireplace there were window seats, and Barry sat down and pulled the curtains aside. "You can see our place from here," he said. "This certainly is a nice lodge, and I'd like to own it."

Kent opened a door from the living room, and they continued to explore. A long hall led to the kitchen at the back of the lodge, and from this hall three bedrooms and a dining room could be reached. It was indeed an unusually large log structure.

"Wouldn't this be a great place to have a party?" Barry exclaimed, with enthusiasm.

"Boy, it surely would!" Kent agreed. He opened a door and looked into one of the bedrooms. "Look at those nice beds, and we are sleeping on the floor over at our cabin!"

Tim called their attention to a pump on the back porch. "Here we are, melting down snow, and a good pump close to us."

"Bet it is frozen stiff," Barry objected.

"Even so, if some hot water were poured down it to prime it, I believe that we could use it," Tim said.

"Well, let's get on upstairs," proposed Barry. "We came over here to see about that window."

They went down the hall and through the living room to the big hall. Barry led the way up the stairs until they came to a door. This was not hard to open, and they found themselves in the attic or loft space of the hunting lodge.

It was a large open space and seemed to be almost empty. A broken bobsled was over against one slope of the roof, and two dusty saddles hung from nails. There were only two windows in the upper section of Bluff Lodge, and one of them was slightly open. Barry crossed the floor of the attic and shut the window, peering out.

"Look at those prints in the snow," he said. "It seems as though someone may have crossed the roof and come in this window. There is enough roof for anyone to walk on."

"Then those tracks were made some time back," reminded Kent. "We haven't had any snow lately. You can see how the snow melted down into the tracks."

"Yes, no doubt of it, the tracks are old," Barry agreed.

Two chimneys rose straight through the attic, and Mac wandered around restlessly. The chimney from the lower hall took up little space, but the living-room chimney rose several feet to push its way through the roof. Mac walked around this brick column while the others looked out of the window toward their cabin.

Then they heard him utter an exclamation. They turned to see him motioning from around the corner of the chimney.

"Come here, you fellows! Look what I've found!"

Filled with curiosity, they joined him behind the tall chimney and found him pointing to a small pile of half-melted snow that showed on the floor. Barry knelt and touched it with his finger.

"It is snow, all right," he announced.

"And that means that somebody has been in the lodge within the last few minutes, possibly while we were walking around downstairs!" Mac reminded them.

CHAPTER X
A Council of War

Somewhat startled at Mac's words, the others looked around the loft and then at each other. The thought that some unknown person had been in the building, perhaps at the same time that they were downstairs, was not a comforting one, and they felt the grip of excitement and uncertainty. Barry glanced up at the roof above them.

"No hole there for this snow to drop through, and we haven't any snow on our shoes," he murmured. "It surely looks like Mac is right."

"If somebody was here, how did he get out?" Tim asked, peering into the dark corners of the loft. "Think he slipped down the roof?"

"It would be easy for anyone to go out the front door while we were in the kitchen," Barry reminded them. "If anybody was hiding in the lodge, he could probably hear us talking and then sneak down into the hall and outdoors while we were in the rear."

"That's just what has happened," Kent exclaimed with conviction.

Barry crushed the snow under his fingers. "It hasn't been here very long," he gave his opinion. "You didn't have any of it on your shoes, did you, Mac?"

The Ford twin shook his head. "No, and I discovered it before I had walked that far. I wasn't sure at first what it was, and I had to touch it to make sure. If that fell off of somebody's clothes, then somebody was here just a few minutes ago."

"Right you are," Kent nodded. "We ought to go down and look through the house again."

"And the sooner the better," seconded Barry, rising from the floor. "I must let Dad know about this."

Led by Kent, the boys went downstairs and made a hasty search through the lodge, but found nothing. It was with considerable excitement that they looked into each room, not at all certain as to what they would find, but no one was in the place. At last they gathered on the front porch and looked up and down the lake, but no one was in sight.

"Let's take a look around the grounds," Tim suggested, and they made a tour of the place. In the rear, back of the kitchen and in a separate building, they found a variety of garden tools and odds and ends, but the shed itself was empty of all life.

The timber came close to the back of the lodge, and if anyone had been bent on vanishing from sight in that direction, it would not have taken him long to do so. Going around on the far side of the lodge, the boys saw that it was more rugged land than that on their side. A series of ravines and gullies ran beside the lodge, and less than an eighth of mile away rose the scarred side of the old abandoned quarry.

"Pretty wild country on this side," said Barry, as they halted under one of the bedroom windows to look around.

Tim approached the gully closest to the house and gazed down into it. "People who camp in this lodge don't want to go walking at night," he said. "Not in this direction, anyway. They had better——Well, I'll be jiggered!"

"What's the matter?" they asked him.

"Looks like our sled down there! It is!"

The others joined him at the edge of the gully. Down below them a few feet they could see the sled, partly turned over, the front runners buried under some snow-laden bushes. Tim slipped down into the depression and located the rope.

"So there is where he hid the sled!" Kent exclaimed.

"And we tramped for miles looking for it!" Barry shook his head.

Tim toiled up the slope, dragging the sled after him. "He did more than hide it there," he informed them, handing the rope to Mac to pull. "Whoever put it there just threw it in. One front runner is broken."

Barry helped Mac pull the sled up. It was a low flat wooden affair with steel runners. Part of the wood over the front runner had been smashed.

"Some nerve on the part of whoever did it," growled Barry, as they examined it. "I'd like to knock the stuffing out of the man!"

"Provided a man did it," Kent said.

"Well, somebody did it, and I suppose it is the same one who has been prowling around this lodge. I mean to find this ghost or whatever it is that is making the trouble at this place."

"It looks as though we ought to do some watching at night," Mac suggested, as they made their way around to the front of the lodge.

"We'll talk it over a little later," Barry promised, locking the front door of the lodge. "We've got to get our firewood in and prepare for the night. These days are short."

Cutting wood and preparing for the night took them the rest of the brief winter afternoon, and then supper followed. The sun had gone down a dull and misty red, and the wind was moaning through the trees. There was every indication of a storm, and the boys were hoping that they would not be snowed in.

"I'll put a splice on that broken sled runner," Kent offered, as they sat at the supper table. He was the best carpenter of them all, and they were willing to let him do the mending.

"All right," Barry agreed. "That will fix it so that we can use it on the way home. Whoever took our sled didn't steal the canvas or the frying pan and the long coffee-pot handle, so he must have taken it just to scare us off."

"He just gave the sled a polite boot into the gully," grumbled Mac.

"Yes, and that gets under my skin," cried Barry. "He came and stole our sled before he knew why we had come here to camp. I wouldn't think so much of it if he had done that after we had been through the lodge, but he didn't even give us that long. Something has got to be done, and we might just as well decide what it will be right here at this council of war."

"Maybe we ought to take turns sitting up and looking out of the window," Mac gave as his idea.

"A pretty cold, thankless job," Kent shook his head. "Hang it all, we didn't do a thing today about making better beds, and so far I haven't enjoyed my sleep."

"I'll tell you what I have been thinking," Barry said slowly. "I believe that we ought to move into the lodge."

There was a moment of silence as the others considered his words, slightly startled at the proposition. "But your Dad told you that he wanted us to stay in this cabin," Tim reminded.

"Yes, he did at that time," Barry agreed. "But the whole situation has changed since then. If we are to get on the track of the mysterious spook of the lodge, we won't do it from here. We ought to be right inside of that hunting lodge."

Again the boys were silent, considering it. "I know that we will be a whole lot more comfortable on those beds over there than we are here," Kent said.

"We'll be a lot better off in several ways," Barry pointed out. "It is a bigger place, and we'll have more elbow room. Then we'll be closer to the actual scene of His Majesty the Spook's activity."

"That spook gets snow on him, same as any human," grinned Mac.

"Of course," nodded Barry. "Because he is human. It's just some mean person up to a slippery game, but who it is or why he is at it, nobody knows. And if we are going to find out, we'll have to hustle, because our time here is going by fast."

"Let's move over there tonight!" Tim suggested.

For a moment they were swayed by the thought, and then Kent and Barry shook their heads together. "Too much of a job at this time of night," Kent said.

"We haven't much to move," Tim protested.

"That's true," Barry agreed. "But the lodge is too cold. We'll have to spend a full day warming up the place. We have only two lanterns, and while I noticed some lamps over there, I don't know whether they have any oil in them or not. We'll do better to wait until morning."

"Taking it by and large, I believe it is the best thing to do," commented Mac. "This little cabin does very well as a shelter from the storm, but it isn't very comfortable."

"It hasn't been well taken care of," answered Kent, looking around. "Some of the chinking is out between the logs, and that lets the air in. This table is thick with grease and looks like it never was cleaned."

"Mr. Bronson has been renting it out for a long time," explained Barry. He got up from the table. "After we have washed the dishes I'll write a letter to my father and tell him that we have decided to move into the lodge—in fact, I'll tell him everything. He might even run up here himself."

56

"I hope we know something more definite by the time he does," observed Mac.

Later in the evening Barry wrote a letter to his father relating events in detail and informing him of their contemplated move. While he was busily engaged at this, the other three boys were working on the broken runner board. Kent had decided to cut out a new one from a piece of board which he had found in the kitchen, and with the aid of ax and knife he managed to carve out a fair section of runner board. With the help of the twins he fitted it into place, and before long the job had been successfully completed.

Before they retired for the night Barry opened the door of the cabin and was surprised to see the soft white flakes falling. "It's snowing," he told his chums.

"Looks as though we are going to move into the lodge just in time," Kent predicted.

"I hope that this doesn't turn into a blizzard," Barry thought.

CHAPTER XI
A Disturbed Night

The sight of the falling snow gave the boys a new channel for conversation, and they were slow about going to bed. They had put everything soft that they could find under their sleeping bags and looked forward to a fairly comfortable night in the log cabin. Since the snow had begun falling the air had become much warmer, and the inside of the little building was warm and inviting.

"It's a thick, heavy snow," Tim remarked, after peering out of the window.

"If anyone comes near the cabin tonight, we ought to see his footprints in the morning," Mac said.

"Maybe not," Kent denied. "If it keeps on snowing this way, any tracks would be covered up in a very short time."

"If it kept up this way for a long time, we'd be snowed in here for a while," Barry told them. "We might not get back to school in time."

"That would break my heart!" Mac grinned.

"Don't you want to know anything, you ignorant duffer?" Kent asked.

"I thought I knew about all there was to know," Mac returned blandly.

"Then you're smarter than most humans," Barry retorted.

"I accept!" grinned the twin.

"We'll ask Pa about that sometime," said Tim, slipping inside the bag. "I bet he'll have a different answer."

The fire blazed up in the chimney, and the shadows leaped and darted on the walls. A split log popped, and a blazing ember shot out across the hearth and landed close to Kent's sleeping bag. He put his arm outside of the bag and flicked it back into the fireplace.

"If any of you get hot in the night, you'll know that a spark landed on you," he said.

"If you know so much, what made that wood pop like that?" Barry asked Mac.

"Expansion. Heat expanded it and made it burst."

"All right. What made that popping sound?"

"That is a secret that we scientific men keep to ourselves," answered Mac soberly.

"I wish you'd all quit talking about such nonsense and let me go to sleep," grumbled Kent. "I'm tired after our tramping around today."

"Yes, let's go to sleep," Mac urged. "Tomorrow I'll explain all these deep things to you!"

"Thanks!" said Barry. "We can hardly wait until we hear them!"

The others were as tired as Kent, and they were willing to drop their good-natured conversation and drift off into slumber. Nor did it take them long. They were active and healthy boys, and sleep was a thing that they needed and enjoyed. In a few moments they were all breathing deeply, and quiet settled over the Bronson cabin.

The fire continued to flare, and occasionally it popped, but no more embers left the chimney. The snow came down gently and settled on the frame of the window until the little panes became round from the clinging white flakes. The wind was rising slightly, and now and then a puff came down the chimney and caused the fire to leap and twist upward.

The slumbers of the mystery hunters were rudely broken into by a sudden medley of shots and yells. The boys woke up with a start, and as they did so two more shots rang out. Then stillness succeeded.

"What was that?" Barry asked, as they sat up in the bags and looked around in the semigloom. The fire had sunk down, and a glance at an old alarm clock that Kent had brought with him, and which stood on the stone chimneypiece, showed that it was a quarter of two.

"Shots," was Kent's answer, as he kicked his way out of the bag. "Several of them, and close to here, too."

"I heard some yells," put in Tim.

All four of them were now up and hastening into their clothes. Mac swiftly tossed some wood on the fire, and in the increasing light they hurriedly dressed. Barry peered out of the window as he pulled his sweater down.

"I don't see anybody," he said. "It is still snowing."

Kent took his rifle from a nail upon which he had hung it, and handed Barry his. "I guess we had better take these with us," he said. "No knowing who is out there, shooting around."

"From the yells we heard, it sounds as though somebody was winged," Mac said, as he took the shotgun that the twins shared between them. Tim placed his ax in his belt, and they were ready to go out into the night and investigate.

Barry opened the door, and they stepped out. It was still snowing, but the flakes were finer now, and there was a brisk wind that moaned through the tops of the trees and whipped the snow into whirling shapes and formations. The boys left the cabin cautiously, but no one challenged their coming, and they stood in the snow outside the door, their hands in pockets, feeling the change from the warm inside to the cold outdoors. Much snow had fallen since they had gone to bed.

For a moment they were silent, listening for any sound that might break the stillness or rise above the gusts of wind, but although they strained their powers of hearing, no sound reached them. Then a flash of light out on the lake caught their attention. It lingered only a moment and then was gone, and after a brief interval, it came again.

"Somebody is running across the ice!" Barry and Mac said in chorus.

"Yes," Kent agreed. "And they have a flashlight that they are turning on every once in a while. Wonder who they are?"

"I'll bet they are the ones that yelled," said Tim.

"Heading for Rake Island," Barry observed.

"Maybe whoever is putting on all the funny business around the lodge hides away on Rake Island," Kent suggested. "We ought to search that place one of these days."

"We will," Barry promised. He glanced toward the dark hunting lodge. "Which way did those shots come from?"

"I'd say from just behind the lodge," Tim answered.

"Seemed that way to me," Kent agreed. "They were mighty close to this cabin of ours."

"Let's go over there and see if we can find anything," Barry suggested.

61

"I'll get the lantern," Mac offered. "You fellows want your hats and gloves?"

They agreed heartily that they did, for the night air was penetrating, and before long the sandy-haired twin was back with the lantern and their warmer clothing. In a short time they set out across the open space toward the lodge, keeping a sharp watch on every side. The flashes no longer came from the lake.

Back of the lodge they flashed the lantern around the ground, looking for footprints, but the snow had been blown around in such a way as to make it impossible for them to find any. They did not waste many minutes in the hunt, as the cold was too keen, but soon gave it up and started back to the cabin.

"Nothing doing," Barry announced. "And I'm not going to stay out here long. That wind feels like a knife. Me for the fire!"

His companions were of the same mind, and they were approaching the cabin when Tim stopped and fumbled into the snow. When he straightened up he held an object in his hand, and as soon as he had wiped it off he whistled.

"Hey! Look here, fellows. A rifle shell!"

The boys bent over his extended hand and examined the metal cartridge with interest. Then Kent began to brush through the snow in search of others. Before long he had found three more.

"This is where the fellow stood that fired those shots," he announced.

"Pretty close to our cabin," Barry said.

"These shells came out of a big rifle," Mac observed. "Did you see that shell on the ground, Tim?"

"No, my foot struck it. I felt something harder than the snow, and I reached down to see what it was. As soon as I touched it, I had an idea what it was."

Barry looked away in the direction of Rake Island, shrouded in the darkness. "It all means that somebody stood here and fired at least four shots from a rifle at someone else," he said slowly. "The ones who were shot at scuttled away across the ice. I'd like to know what it all means."

62

"Let's get in around the fire and look these shells over," Kent urged, and they were soon back in the cabin, grouping around the warm fire and looking at the empty cartridge curiously. The ones that Kent had found were exactly the same, and there was no doubt that they had all been shot from the same gun.

"It seemed to me that there were more than four shots, but perhaps I just imagined that," Barry said, sitting down on the sleeping bag.

"The whole thing was so sudden and unexpected that I hardly know what did happen," Mac admitted. "The shots were near us, too."

"Almost outside of our window," Kent nodded. "Gosh, that gives me something to think about, do you know it? The light of our fire would show anyone that we were here, and whoever fired the shots might have been protecting us. See what I mean?"

"Do you mean that those people who ran across the ice may have been looking in at us and were scared off by the shots?" Tim asked.

"Sure! Or maybe the ones who did the shooting were looking in at us and were disturbed. Of course, any way you look at it, it is all pure guesswork, and we know as much about it as we do about the whole mystery business."

"I'm glad that we are going to move over into the lodge," declared Barry. "That's a bigger place, and I'll feel safer in it."

"Don't forget, though, that the lodge is the home stamping ground for the spook," Mac reminded him.

"I know it is, but we seem to have had a lot of visitors and prowlers around here. I don't feel quite safe any more. If we did stay in this cabin, we'd have to build some sort of a shutter to put over that window, so that people couldn't come looking in."

"Do you believe it was any of Carter Wolf's friends?" Tim inquired.

Barry smiled. "We're trying to hang everything against his account, just because he has no use for us. No, I hardly think so. I wonder if any of his bunch carries a rifle big enough for these shells?"

"They might," Kent said. "Some of his friends are sports and have good equipment. We know that he is somewhere near here, but I just don't think that they had anything to do with it all."

"Well, that artillery practice was too close to suit me," Mac declared, as he began to get ready for bed again.

"I'm just wondering if anyone was hit or if they just yelled because they were scared," murmured Barry, as the boys prepared to go to sleep again.

"I suppose we should have gone on down to the lake to see if anyone was hurt or not," admitted Tim.

Mac placed fresh fuel on the fire, and they talked for another half-hour about the mysterious event of the night. The wind was rising and blowing more strongly, and the old cabin shook under the force of some of the blasts. At length the boys became quiet and sank away into deep sleep.

It seemed that they had scarcely closed their eyes when there came a thunderous booming crash that jarred the cabin. Something scraped down the roof and fell to the ground back of the lean-to kitchen. At the same time some stones fell into the fire, which had sunk to red embers, scattering it to right and left. The boys bounded up from their beds with rapidly beating hearts.

"What was that?" Tim shouted.

"Something hit the cabin," Barry said, as he reached for his clothes again.

"Yes, and it took part of the chimney," Mac pointed out. "I'll get a light and we'll see what it was."

Kent threw the remaining wood on the fire, and Mac lighted the lantern. It was just five o'clock, an hour which rather surprised the boys, as it was still pitch dark outside. They dressed as quickly as possible, waiting for further sounds, but all was still.

"Do you suppose that somebody bumped against the side of the cabin?" Mac asked.

"Bumped it with a battering ram if he did," Barry retorted. "That thump was on the roof. Let's see what it was."

He seized the lantern, and the others followed him out into the early-morning air. The blackness was growing faintly gray in the east, and before very long the sun would be up. But the boys were not interested in these things at that moment. They walked out to a place where they could look at the roof of the cabin.

One glance told the story. A big limb had blown down and landed on the roof, knocking off a corner of the chimney. Part of the limb had slid down the back part of the roof, but the heaviest portion was still balanced on the peak of the roof.

"A tree limb!" Kent cried. "We might have known it."

"A big one, too," Barry observed. "We'll have to pull it down before we leave this cabin."

"I thought the whole house was coming down when it hit," Mac grinned.

"Are you going to go back to sleep?" Tim inquired.

"Sleep?" echoed Kent, in disgust. "Not for me! It's morning, anyway. If we did go to sleep, something else would be sure to happen. I'm sleepy, but no more for me. What a fine night that turned out to be!"

CHAPTER XII
A Surprise Visit

Satisfied by their inspection, the boys now went back into the cabin and began to fix things in order. All of them felt sleepy and somewhat dragged out, but in no mood to return to the sleeping bags. Faint streaks of real daylight were spread across the sky, and a new day was at hand.

It was still snowing lightly, and the wind was cutting and sharp. Before long it was evident that there would be no sunshine that day. The sky was heavy and overcast. The trees were loaded with a mass of clinging white flakes, and the whole landscape was clothed in a simple beauty that the boys admired with enthusiasm.

"If the sun would come out, how this snow would flash and sparkle!" Kent remarked, as they tucked away the bedding and prepared to get breakfast.

"No sun today," Barry predicted. "In fact, I wouldn't be surprised if we have more snow."

"Going to move over into that lodge this morning?" Mac inquired.

"I guess so," Barry nodded. "But first we want to go down to the lake and see if we can find any clues to what went on last night."

"We ought to scout around a little and see if we can find anyone in the woods who did the shooting," Tim suggested.

"We'll do the best we can," Barry assured them. "I want to get to the post office at Fox Point and mail my letter to Dad. We won't be here much longer."

"No, we won't, worse luck," sighed Kent. "I'd like to stay right here until we do solve the mystery."

"Looks like we aren't going to," Mac shook his head. "It gets deeper all the time."

"Somebody has got to get more wood," Tim called from the lean-to. "Who are the brave lads who will volunteer to chop or die for their native land?"

"I'm brave, but this isn't my native land," Barry grinned.

"You'd better do it, Tim," Mac suggested. "You're always carrying a little hatchet around in your belt."

"That's no hatchet, that happens to be an ax," growled Tim. "I'm all set to cook breakfast, and as it is going to be a tough job to cut wood under the snow, I'm calling for volunteers!"

"He's honest about it," commented Barry. "It is hard work, so he wants somebody else to do it."

"I'll do the chopping," Kent said suddenly. "Come on, Mac, you go with me."

Mac stared at him suspiciously. "You seem mighty anxious. Where are you going to find a log to cut into?"

"Upon the roof, my boy," grinned Kent. "All we have to do is to toss a rope up and snake it down. Once it descends to the ground, we will fall on it tooth and nail and reduce it to kindling wood!"

Mac seized his ax with alacrity. "And that means that the next time wood is cut, those two have to cut it wherever they can find it, doesn't it? That's fine! Let's go!"

"We're sold," Barry smiled at Tim. "The boys have put one over on us."

Mac and Kent went to work at once on the limb that hung over the peak of the roof. Standing on Kent's shoulders, the twin looped a rope over a jagged stump of a limb and then jumped to the ground. Both of them pulled on the rope and the limb came sliding down the roof and thudded to the ground.

"A good, dry piece of timber," Kent exulted. "This will be easy to chop up for firewood."

They fell to their task with a will and soon had an ever-growing pile heaped up close to the front door. Barry came out to get some of it, and Tim started the fire in the rusty stove. Before long the delicious smell of bacon drifted out to the wood-choppers. Mac stopped and sniffed with rapture.

"Boy, just smell that bacon! Isn't that the finest aroma in the world?"

"It certainly is when you are out camping," Kent granted. "Everything seems to taste so good when you are out in the open a whole lot."

"Bacon, eggs, and coffee! What a combination! Say, while you fellows are at Fox Point today, why don't you get some sausage?"

"We'll ask Barry, or whoever goes, to get it."

Breakfast was soon ready, and they tackled it with enthusiasm. Just as soon as the meal was over they set the cabin in order. All of them were anxious to get out and explore the lake front, but they were good campers and had an instinctive aversion to leaving the camp until it was in first-class condition. This was speedily done, and then they donned their outside coats and their hats and were ready to go.

"Taking guns?" Kent asked.

"Might as well," Barry said. "Not that we expect to use them for defensive purposes, but we might see some game that we can knock over."

They left the cabin and locked the door after them. "Nothing in there of value except our provisions, skates, and sled," Mac remarked. "But I suppose it is best to lock up."

"We'll explore a little and then get back to our moving," Barry proposed, as they plodded along through the snow down the slope to the lake. "We don't want to spend another night in the Bronson cabin."

They soon reached the shore of the lake and searched it for footprints or other clues, but were unable to find anything. Proceeding along the edge of the frozen water, they hiked almost as far east as the mouth of the Buffalo River. When they were opposite Rake Island, Kent came to an abrupt halt and pointed.

"Look, some fellows are on Rake Island. See them watching us?"

Glancing across the ice sheet, they saw five figures standing in a group, apparently looking in their direction. Just as they noticed them, the group on the little island started across the lake toward them. The boys at once halted.

"They are coming right at us," Barry remarked.

"Doesn't it look like Carter Wolf in the lead?" Tim asked.

Kent nodded. "Just what I thought. We're in for trouble."

"Five to four," murmured Mac.

"Hold your horses," Barry advised. "We don't know what they want, and besides that we have guns and they haven't anything in their hands. Don't let them get near enough to take anything away from you. Maybe they only want to buy something."

"I can't very well picture Carter Wolf wanting to buy anything from us," Kent shook his head.

The members of the island camp soon drew close to them, and there was no doubt that it was Carter Wolf and some of his friends from a neighboring town. These boys were expensively dressed, and Wolf wore a big fur coat and hat that looked odd as a camping outfit. They carried no weapons with them, and it was impossible to imagine what their object was.

They approached the mystery hunters, and the silence between the two groups was strained. Barry decided to make the advances.

"Good-morning," he greeted.

The other boys made no answer, but they slowed up and finally stopped a few feet away. Wolf's face wore a frown, and his companions stood slightly in back of him. They were all boys who did not look especially healthy, and the boys from the cabin knew that they were all drinkers and considered themselves to be good sports.

"You tried pretty hard to hit us last night, didn't you?" Wolf began aggressively.

"We didn't have anything to do with whatever happened last night," Barry answered him. "You'll have to tell us all about it."

"We believe that," sneered Wolf. "Just because you saw us sitting on the porch of that lodge, you blazed away at us. I can have you arrested for that."

Kent looked at him coldly. "The fact of the matter, Wolf, is that we were asleep in the Bronson cabin at the time that shooting happened. We got dressed and came out as soon as we could, and you and your friends were running across the ice. We didn't have a thing to do with it."

"I suppose I'm to believe it or not," scoffed the boy from the island.

Tim dug down into his Mackinaw pocket. "I guess we can soon settle that question," he said. "Here are the empty shells that we picked up outside our cabin after the shooting. You can see that they are far

70

too big for our little rifles, and you know that it wasn't a shotgun that was fired at you. Need any further proof?"

It was evident that the boys from Rake Island did not, but they were in anything but a pleasant frame of mind. They were anxious to make trouble but had no ground to stand on. Wolf tried a new line of attack.

"Your father has charge of that lodge," he accused Barry. "If anything had happened to us, he would have been responsible. We had been up the lake to a dance hall and came back late. All we did was to sit down on the porch of the lodge because Hodge here was unsteady——"

"Don't be telling all you know," spoke up a boy with a pasty, unhealthy-looking face.

"Well, anyway, somebody shot at us," Wolf went on. "If we had been hit, your father would have had to pay for it."

"I don't think so," Barry denied. "I guess you know that the lodge has the name of being haunted, and you were taking your own chances when you sat on the porch."

"Some fine day our bunch will go up there and crash in," Wolf boasted. "We'll see what all this ghost business is."

"If you can find out what it is, my father will be grateful to you," Barry assured him. "But I wouldn't crash into the lodge, if I were in your place."

"Don't give me advice, Garrison! I don't need any, and if I did, I wouldn't come to you for it. You know that if I ever get a chance to square accounts with you, I'm going to!"

"You haven't any account to square," Barry returned levelly. "You just think you have. We're not looking for any trouble with you, Wolf, and the farther you stay away from us, the better we'll like it!"

"I think we ought to give you fellows a good beating," cried Wolf, starting forward. But a companion named Carl Voss pulled him back quickly.

"Come on back to camp and leave these kids alone," he advised, his eyes upon the weapons hanging across the boys' arms. "They didn't shoot at us."

Wolf allowed himself to be dragged away, but his eyes were sullen and revengeful. "Some day it will be my turn to crow," was his parting word.

"Looks like you're doing all the crowing right now," murmured Tim, as they watched the other party start back to the island.

CHAPTER XIII
In the Grip of the Storm

For a few moments the boys from the cabin camp watched the Rake Island boys walk across the ice, and then Barry turned away. "Come on," he said. "We haven't time to stand around idle. Remember that we want to move today, and already we have spent a good part of the morning."

The other followed him, and they started back to the camp. "We've learned something, anyway," Kent remarked.

"Yes, it was the Wolf bunch that was shot at," Mac nodded.

"Still, we're just as much as ever in the dark as to who did the shooting," Tim reminded them.

"It looks to me as though whoever did the shooting did it to scare them off," said Barry. "They weren't hit and didn't say anything about the shots going overhead. I guess that crowd didn't have anything to do with taking our sled."

"For a while I thought that they did," confessed Kent. "But evidently they didn't know anything about it. Somebody keeps mighty close tabs on the lodge and even objects when anybody sits on the front porch."

"What will they do when we go to live in the place?" Barry asked.

"They may make it warm for us," Tim suggested. "So far we have been living in the Bronson cabin, and they haven't done any more than steal our sled and throw it into a ravine. But now we are moving up on the ghost, and maybe things will get lively."

"Scared?" Mac asked.

"No, but I believe we ought to be prepared for action."

"We will be," Barry agreed. "Perhaps we ought to take turns staying up at night and keeping a strict watch. I have an idea that some dangerous criminal is operating around that lodge."

"I wonder if there are any counterfeiters making money anywhere in the neighborhood," Mac mused.

"It may be," Barry admitted. "Whatever they are, someone doesn't want anybody to hang around the lodge. We'll just have to show them that we intend to stay there."

73

"That's the talk!" Kent approved.

Still discussing the things nearest their minds, the boys arrived at the cabin close to dinner time. After some thought they decided to postpone their moving until the afternoon.

"Tim and I can move the things over, if you and Kent want to go to Fox Point," Mac told Barry.

"I ought to go mail my letter," Barry said. "And we need some things from the store there, kerosene in particular. Our lantern is about empty, and we'll want some oil for the lamps in the lodge."

"Not to forget Mac's sausage," smiled Kent.

"It won't take us any time to move our few things over there," Tim said. "You boys go ahead, and we'll manage the domestic affairs."

This was agreed to, and after the midday meal Kent and Barry prepared to start out. They took the sled with them, but decided not to skate.

"That would be a couple of miles up the lake and then down the river," Kent argued. "We can cut our distance by going through the woods."

"The ice is almost covered with snow anyway," observed Barry. "We can hike it as quickly as we could skate."

Strapping the long kerosene oil container to the sled, they were ready to start out. The twins watched them from the door.

"If you come to a good hill, you can sit on the sled and coast down," Mac grinned.

"That will be all right if you don't run up against a stump," Tim added.

Barry slipped the sled rope through his belt and they were off. "See you in our new quarters before long," he called back.

"Have a warm fire by the time we get there," Kent requested.

"Don't forget coffee and butter!" Tim yelled.

"And sausage!" Mac whooped.

With a laugh and a reassuring wave the two boys with the sled entered the woods and were lost to sight.

Barry and Kent struck off in a southeasterly direction through the woods. They knew that Fox Point lay in that direction and were

74

interested to see how near they would come to it. There was no definite path to follow, and so they wound around bluffs and between the trees, checking their course by a pocket compass. The forest was a fairly open one, and the trees stood well apart, making it easy to draw the sled. Underfoot the snow made a soft carpet.

The entire day had been a gloomy one, and the sky was gray and heavy, with a strong hint of snow in it. Darkness would come quickly, and the two boys were aware of the fact and determined to lose no time in making the trip.

"If we push on at a fast pace, we should be back at the lodge before it gets dark," Kent said, as they crossed a brook and started up a hill slope.

"We won't linger in the store," Barry promised. "It will be dark earlier than usual tonight, and we'll have to make a flying trip of it. I suppose we should have started out this morning."

"I guess so, if we had wanted to take our time about it. Oh, well, I'm sure that we'll make it all right. Beginning to snow, isn't it?"

Kent was right. Lazy flakes of snow began to drift down through the trees, and when they reached the top of the hill they could see for some distance. In every direction the air was filled with softly falling flakes.

"If it doesn't come down any harder than that, it won't bother us any," Kent remarked.

"Hard to tell about that," his companion said. "Some pretty hard storms start out mildly. Those clouds above look to be full. However, we won't borrow trouble until we have to."

They crossed a somewhat thicker section of timber and came to the top of another rise of ground. Barry pointed ahead of them.

"See that church steeple? I believe that is Fox Point."

"If it is, we've hit it pretty well. It won't be long before we know for certain."

They set off once more and before long came to the edge of the woods and saw the little crossroads village of Fox Point before them. A few houses, a general store, and a church and school building made up the tiny country village. The boys went at once to the store and, leaving the sled outside, were soon warming their hands at the big iron stove in the center of the store.

Then Barry began to order supplies, and Kent wandered to the window, looking down into the road. Presently he called to his companion.

"I wonder if that is the French couple that Mac and Tim saw?"

Barry joined him at the window and looked down. Two horses were tied to a railing at a water trough which was empty, and as the boys looked out at the scene, a man and woman got on the horses. Barry recognized the man at once.

"Yes, that is the fellow who came into our camp that morning," he said.

Filled with curiosity, the storekeeper came over and joined them at the window. The boys watched the French couple ride off and enter a path that led into the woods below the town.

"Those people been around these parts a few days," the owner of the store confided. "You acquainted with them?"

"No, but early one morning the man was standing looking over our camp," Barry told him. "Two of our friends visited them in their camp once, but we don't know anything about them. Do you?"

The storekeeper went around the counter and began to tie up packages. "I know they are mighty mysterious people. Won't say who they are or what they want. The other night they come in the store and I asked them what I could do for them. Said they didn't want nothin' but to wait for somebody. Pretty soon a car come along and blowed the horn outside and they went out to it, and that was the last I see of them until today. Nobody knows anything about 'em."

"They didn't have any rifles today," Barry said to Kent, when the storekeeper had moved off.

"I noticed that. They must have settled somewhere to stay." Kent chuckled. "I'll bet it hurts these people not to know what they are doing here."

The packages were soon ready, and the boys took them out and tied them in place. Over the top they spread the canvas to keep the snow out, and then they were ready. Barry looked around and then shook his head.

"It is beginning to snow harder and faster," he said. "We'll have to step right along."

Leaving Fox Point behind them, the two boys started off through the woods toward Bluff Lodge, striding along as fast as they could. The snow was coming down hard, and before they had gone two miles it was blinding. The two chums said very little, but both of them were apprehensive as the sky grew darker and the whirling flakes more bewildering. Their clothing became white.

"We got into a good one this time," Barry called to Kent, as they rounded a high rocky ledge.

"You're right! Say, did we pass that ledge on the way to Fox Point?"

"I think so. Hang it all, I can hardly see anything."

They pressed on, picturing the twins in the lodge with a warm and glowing fire to welcome them. The loaded sled was a trifle heavy owing to the opposition of the increasing depth of snow, and they relieved each other frequently.

They had traveled on for over a half-hour, peering through the storm and almost feeling their way, when Kent stopped and pointed.

"Look! There is that same ledge. We've come around in a complete circle!"

Barry nodded bitterly. "We have. I hate to admit it, but we're just lost! And if you ask me, we've managed to get lost at a mighty serious time!"

CHAPTER XIV
New Quarters

The twins watched the departure of their chums and then turned back into the house. Mac closed the door and walked over to the fire, rubbing his hands.

"It doesn't do to get far away from the fire these days," he grinned.

"Not for long," his brother admitted. "We had better get over to the lodge and start a fire there. That place is going to be cold."

"Yes, and it will take some time to warm it up, too. Did Barry leave the key?"

Tim took it from his pocket. "Here it is. Let's take some of the stuff and go on over there."

They put on coats and hats and, taking a few things with them, left the Bronson cabin and crossed to the lodge. Tim unlocked the front door of Bluff Lodge, and they went in. The interior of the lodge was cold, and their breath stood out in dense white clouds. Without lingering in the hall they went directly to the big living room and put their equipment on the window seats.

"The first thing we had better do," Mac suggested, "is to get the fire going. This fireplace looks like a good one, and it shouldn't take long. Want to put paper in while I go haul a load of wood on the sled?"

"We haven't got the sled," Tim reminded him. "Barry and Kent have it, so you'll have to carry some over."

"That's so, I had forgotten. They took the sled to bring home the well-known bacon."

"Or your sausage," Tim grinned.

"It won't be mine alone. You know that you like it yourself and so do the other boys. Well, I'll be back in a few seconds with some wood."

"We haven't got much of it," Tim said. "We'll have to cut some more."

"I know it. That is the biggest job we have."

Mac left the lodge, and Tim busied himself piling some newspaper which he had brought in the fireplace. There were some ashes left from a previous fire, and he cleaned them out and carried them in a pail to the kitchen, where he unlocked the back door and took the pail out to where the bushes grew in a wild tangle. Here he dumped the ashes and then looked around. The door of the Bronson cabin was open, and he could see Mac inside.

Returning to the lodge, his eyes lighted on a small shed joined to the kitchen. It was one part of the lodge that they had not inspected, and his curiosity was aroused.

"Wonder what that place is. But I suppose it is locked up."

He tried the knob on the door that led to the small shed and found that it was locked. The key ring for the lodge was still in his pocket, and he took it out, examining the keys closely.

"The key to this shed may be on the ring. Nothing like trying."

He fitted two keys to the lock on the shed, and the second one fitted. One turn and the lock slipped back. He pulled the door open and peered inside. Then he gave a whistle of surprise and pleasure.

"Coal, by ginger! Half a shed full of coal. I must tell Mac about this."

He did not linger long out in the crisp air, but returned to the living room of the hunting lodge. Just as he reached the fireplace, Mac came in with a load of wood.

"This is the last of it," he announced. "We'll have to cut some more before it gets dark, and we'll have to hustle to it because it is getting darker all the time. We're in for a storm."

"We'll have to cut some wood," Tim told him. "But I made a great discovery, Mac. There is a shed joined to the kitchen, and it is half filled with coal. That means an end to our wood-chopping."

"It doesn't belong to us," Mac interposed, practically.

"I know, but if we pay for what we use, it ought to be all right. In the little time left for us to stay here we won't use much. Come on and look at it."

He led his brother to the coal shed, and Mac inspected it. "I suppose it will be all right," the sandy-haired twin nodded. "If it isn't, Barry will tell us when he gets back here. At any rate, we can use it to warm up the room in there, and it will do the job quicker than wood will. Let's take a bucket of it in the house."

80

"This coal explains why they use grates in the hall and the living room," Tim said, as they filled a coal pail that hung close by.

Returning to the living room of the lodge, they quickly built the fire. The flames licked their way up through the paper and over the wood, and when this had caught fire in good style they put some coal on. As the fire blazed out in a comforting manner, the brothers stood and watched it with satisfaction.

"The first fire in this room for many a day," remarked Tim.

Mac grinned. "That ghost or spook must be a cold-blooded fellow, prowling around here in rooms as cold as these are."

Tim glanced out of the window. "Mac, it is snowing again, and I have a hunch that it is going to snow hard. Let's get some more wood in before things close down."

"I guess we had better. Some of that limb over at the cabin is left, and we can get our supply off of that."

The twins took their axes and hastened to the limb before the cabin. Falling to with a will, they soon had the wood supply mounting. The storm increased as they worked, until they could scarcely see for the whirling flakes. For some time they were silent, saving their energy for the task before them, but their minds were on the same subject. Mac leaned on his ax for a breathing spell.

"I'm afraid that the boys will have a hard time finding their way through this storm," he said.

Tim stopped chopping and looked anxiously toward the forest, which could barely be seen. Both boys had a goodly quantity of snow on their shoulders and hats.

"I have been thinking the same thing," he admitted. "You can hardly see the woods from here. And they don't know the way very well."

"Maybe they can see better in the woods than we can out here in the open," said Mac hopefully. He began to chop again with vigor. "Let's get through here and get back in the lodge. By golly, we can hardly see anything ourselves, and we might get lost without much trouble!"

They carried their wood into the lodge and then returned to the cabin for a final load of their camping equipment. Satisfied that they now had everything, Tim locked the door and trotted across the open space to the hunting lodge. He paused at the door for a final look at the white, storm-tossed world about him, and an anxious frown gathered on his forehead.

"How I wish Kent and Barry were back here! I don't see how they can possibly find their way in a storm like this one."

More troubled than he cared to admit, Tim joined his twin before the fire in the large grate. "Might as well take off our coats and make ourselves at home, hadn't we?" he asked.

"I was just thinking about priming that pump on the back porch. I'm tired of snow water."

"So am I. But I'm afraid that pump is frozen solid."

"No doubt of it, but some good hot water poured in it ought to break it loose. It is warmer today than it has been most of the time. Want to try it?"

"I guess so. How will we heat water? There is nothing to hang a kettle on."

Mac examined the fireplace closely. "No, there isn't. But we could set the kettle right on the coals. Wouldn't hurt the kettle any."

"Let's look in the kitchen and see what we can find there," Tim proposed. "We could start a fire in the stove and heat our water there."

"I guess we had better not use up our wood on a kitchen fire," Mac shook his head. "For tonight we can get along with this grate fire. We don't know how long this storm will last, so we will have to be careful."

They traversed the long hall to the kitchen and examined the pots and pans that hung on hooks under the shelves. From the closet beside the cook range Mac brought out a curiously shaped pan. It was flat on one side and had a long handle to it. A hook curved out from the flat side, and there was a hinged cover for it.

"What the dickens kind of a pot is this, Tim? I never saw one like it before."

Tim looked it over with interest. "Hanged if I know," he began, then suddenly his face lighted up. "Why, Mac, this must be a pan to hang on the grate. This hook goes over the top grate bar, and you can heat water in it. Just the thing we need!"

"That's just exactly what it is," Mac nodded. "I'll get some snow, and we can melt it down and then try our luck on that pump."

They filled the grate pan with snow and then took it in and hooked it on the top bar of the grate. There was now no doubt in their minds that the utensil was meant for its present use.

"While that is melting and heating, let's get the lamps in here," Tim suggested, and they brought the oil lamps in from the bedrooms. There was very little oil left in them, and the boys had only a scanty supply in their lanterns.

"We'll have plenty when Barry and Kent get here," Mac remarked, looking out at the storm. But the scene that met his eye was not a reassuring one. If anything, the storm was increasing.

"That snow has melted down and will soon be hot water," Tim said, after a glance into the grate pan. "Guess we'd better get another pan of snow and keep melting it, because that pump will have to be primed more than once."

This was done, and as the water became hot the boys kept adding snow. At last the pan was filled with boiling water, and they poured it into the tea kettle, and after refilling the grate pan with snow they set off for the back porch to try their luck with the pump. Tim carefully poured the boiling fluid down the neck of the rusty iron pump shaft. Steam arose as the hot water came in contact with the ice.

"If we do get this thing going, we'll have to prime it every morning," Mac predicted, standing first on one foot and then on the other and moving about to keep warm.

"Yes, no doubt of that. Gosh, it is getting colder. Good thing this porch shelters us from some of the wind."

They poured pan after pan of boiling water down the pump shaft without attaining the end they were seeking, and were about to give it up as a bad job, when Mac felt the pump handle move with a sucking sound. He pressed harder.

"I think she's coming!" he cried. "Put another dose in."

Tim did so, and the water came pouring up, bringing with it a mixture of ice and rust flakes. The brothers worked the handle vigorously, and soon a stream of clear water flowed out.

"Hurrah, we made it," Tim exulted. "Thought we weren't going to, though."

"So did I. That water looks good. Wait until I get a glass from the kitchen, and we can have a good drink of it."

They filled some pails with the water and then returned to the house. Darkness was beginning to settle, and their spirits became more and more depressed. It was close to five o'clock, and the blackness of night soon closed entirely over the lodge. Tim lighted a lamp, and they were comfortable as far as light and warmth were concerned. But their minds were far from easy.

"No use talking, the boys have either stayed at Fox Point or they are lost," Mac sighed, as they looked out of the window into the thick blackness.

"I don't believe they stayed," Tim shook his head. "I'm afraid that they started on the return trip and got caught. The tough part is that if we go out to look for them, we would probably be lost in a short time, too!"

CHAPTER XV
Mysterious Knocking

For a moment after Tim's discouraging words the twins stood and stared helplessly out at the darkness of the night. From every angle the situation was a serious one. If the country had been familiar to them, they would have attempted to go out and look for Barry and Kent, but they had only a sketchy notion of the hills and valleys. The wind was blowing the snow around in such a way that even the stoutest woodsmen might have been confused and lost on such a day. To the Ford boys it seemed anything but cheering that their chums were somewhere abroad in the storm and darkness.

"I wish I knew what to do," Mac confessed, after they had stared out into the night for some time.

Tim turned from the window and took off his hat and coat. "The first thing we had better do is to get our things off," he recommended. "It is getting mighty warm in here now. Then we had better get supper ready. They might come in yet, Mac. Maybe we're only borrowing trouble."

"It may be," his brother agreed, brightening up. "They may have waited at Fox Point until it blew over and will be here later. But if this keeps up, they'll have to come here on snowshoes."

"Yes, it is getting deep. Well, what shall we do about supper? We aren't going to build a kitchen fire, and we won't eat in that big dining room."

"No, we can make this room our headquarters for about everything," Mac nodded. "Let's bring in that table from the kitchen and set it right here by the fire. It will just fit our needs."

Willing to occupy their minds with something besides worry, the two boys went to the kitchen and carried out the small table that Mac had spoken about. It was just large enough for the four of them, and they found clean knives and forks in the drawer, but Tim washed them for the sake of safety. After this was done he put them around the table.

"I'll set four places," he said.

Mac glanced at the clock and noted that it was close to six. "Sure, set four places, they'll be along soon," he said, but his voice lacked conviction, and both of them were more alarmed than they would care to admit.

"What shall we have for supper?" Tim inquired, beginning to dig among the stores that they had brought over from the cabin.

"I was hoping to have sausage," Mac smiled. "But I guess we had better not count on it. Open a can of pork and beans. I'll fix the coffee."

For a while they worked silently. The fire was a mass of glowing red coals, and the room was lighted by one lamp. They could see well enough by this light and did not intend to light another one, because they thought it best to save for an emergency. Tim put the beans on to warm, and Mac made coffee. While these things were coming along, the brothers sat on the wicker couch and stared into the fire.

"I hope the other boys aren't cold while we are enjoying this fine fire," Mac murmured.

"They may be around the stove at Fox Point," Tim hoped.

"Sure. On the other hand, we can't help but realize that they may be out in the woods, wandering around. Hang it all, I hate waiting worse than anything else on earth!"

Tim sprang up and went to the window, peering out. "So do I. I wonder——No, the storm is pretty bad, and we had better not get away from the lodge. Listen to that old wind!"

Mac couldn't help listening to it. With a shrill, whistling sound it tore around the lodge and made some of the windows rattle. The fire in the grate was vigorous and glowing because of it. Already the coffee was bubbling, and a tempting odor came from the pot on the coals. Had the other boys been there with them, they would have thoroughly enjoyed it all, but just now its attraction was lost in the air of uncertainty that surrounded them.

"I think we moved out of the cabin just in time," he said. "That little old place is something of an antique, and it was colder than it should have been. I'll bet the wind is coming in under the door over there."

Tim nodded, looking around the room they were in. "Yes, this surely is a great improvement. Wicker couch and chairs, window seats

86

and well-filled bookcases. How shall we sleep tonight? In the bedrooms?"

"I don't think so. Too cold. This couch will be good for one of us to sleep on, and if we lug the mattresses in here, we can make dandy beds. I have an idea that the sheets and everything else in those rooms would be as cold as ice."

Tim took the pan of beans off of the fire. "These are ready, and the boys aren't here yet, though it is after six. Want to eat?"

Mac shook his head. "Not yet. Let's wait awhile. We can heat them up again when they come. I'll go get some more coal."

He put his coat and hat on and took the coal pail. Tim silently handed him the flashlight. Mac went out the door and down the hall, while Tim stared into the fire.

Mac did not stay out long, and when he got back he rubbed his hands. "Man alive, but it is cold! Say, the boys have no lantern with them, have they?"

"No, only a flashlight."

"They couldn't keep a lantern going, anyway, on a windy night like this."

Silence again fell between them, and at last it was seven o'clock. Tim looked around the room and then got up. They had put the lamp out and had been sitting in the light of the fire.

"Mac, they aren't coming, so you and I had better eat something. I know you don't feel much like eating, and neither do I, but it will do us good to pack something solid away inside of us."

"I never felt less like eating," growled Mac.

"I know it. I realize just now how you feel. But we might need our strength later on, and we can do more for the boys on a full stomach than we ever could on an empty one."

"You're right," his brother nodded. "If we only knew something! It is the uncertainty that makes it all so hard."

Once more they warmed the beans and coffee, and when the food had been placed on their plates and the beverage in the cups, they began to eat. It was a hasty and a silent meal, for they were oppressed, and neither of them possessed any appetite to speak of. The two empty places at the table haunted them, and they found it hard to keep various alarming thoughts out of their heads.

"I think we ought to light a lamp and put it in the window, as a guide for them," Mac proposed, when they had finished their meal.

"Sure thing," Tim agreed. "They may come along late, and any kind of a light will be a help to them. We haven't got much oil, but we'll use all that we have in a lamp for them."

Mac picked up a taboret and put it on the window seat. "Put the lamp on top of that," he directed. "That ought to shine for quite a distance. If the oil runs out, we can go until daylight without any. We'll get enough coal in here to last all night, and we won't have to build a new fire in the morning. If they haven't come in by that time we'll have to go after them, storm or no storm." Tim placed the lighted lamp on the taboret, and the boys felt that they had done all that could be done under the circumstances. Mac sat on the couch in a reclining position, and his brother squinted at the titles on the backs of the books in the bookcase.

"I'll try a little reading," he announced. "Don't know how successful it will be."

Mac yawned and slid a little lower. "I'm too tired and worried to read," he said. "Better not get hold of a spook book."

"It wouldn't be a bad idea," Tim replied. "I need something exciting to keep me awake and take my mind off of things."

He finally found a book that suited him, and, drawing a chair close to the lamp on the taboret, he started to read. Mac sank lower on the couch and soon fell asleep. Tim read on. It was a little colder over near the lamp than he wished for, but he didn't want to take the lamp away from the window.

A sudden clear tapping on the window back of him caused Tim to start violently and almost drop his book. It came on the glass of the window at the end of the room and not where the light was. Tim jumped up joyously, sure that the boys had returned.

"Hey, Mac! Wake up! The boys are here!"

Mac bounded to his feet. "They are? Where?"

88

Tim was at the dark window, peering out. "They just knocked here. I can't see them, but they just tapped on the glass while I was reading. Almost scared——There!"

"They are at the back door," Mac whooped, seizing his flashlight. "Come on, we're the committee of welcome."

"We'll surely welcome them," Tim agreed, as they made their way along the hall to the kitchen. Mac quickly turned the key in that door and drew back the knob. The door opened, but no one was there. The boys looked around the porch and flashed the light into every corner, but without success.

"I was sure that knocking came from the back door," Tim exclaimed, when they failed to find anyone.

"So was I. Maybe they are trying to put something over on us."

"Maybe," admitted Tim, doubtfully. "But I should think they would have had enough of being out in the cold. Well, they aren't here. We had better go in. Your flashlight is getting weak."

"It's about shot." Mac locked the door, and they walked slowly down the hall toward the living room. It had just occurred to them that they were in what was known as a haunted lodge, and various thoughts were crowding into their minds. In the living room they looked uncertainly at each other.

"I doubt if the boys would play any such foolish stunts," Tim remarked.

"I doubt it, too. Of course, it's a good opportunity to have a little fun with——"

"Listen!" Tim cried, holding up his hand.

There were three distinct thumps on the side of the lodge, and then all was quiet. Then a loud and insistent knocking came on the front door. The twins looked at each other with startled eyes. Then Tim took the lamp, and they started for the front door. Mac took up the poker as they passed the fireplace.

"I'll open the door," he said, and while Tim held the lamp he turned the key and pulled the knob. The door came open with a rush, and the wind snuffed the lamp flame out in a twinkling, and yet not so quickly that the Ford twins could make out the fact that there was no one near the front door.

CHAPTER XVI
The Quarry Shed

Barry and Kent stood in the storm-tossed woods and gazed with sinking hearts at the ledge of rock before them. It told them in unmistakable terms that they were lost and, as Barry had truly said, at a very serious time. After all of their recent pushing on, they were right back at the place where they had been a short time before.

"I wonder how we came to go around like that?" Kent asked, as he brushed snow from the front of his coat and tried to see around him.

"Easy to do in a blinding storm like this one," Barry replied. "Well, we're into it for fair. Shall we try it again, or turn back to Fox Point?"

"I don't want to turn back," Kent protested. "Mac and Tim will be badly worried, and I'd like to make it through, if we possibly can. Which way do you think we ought to go?"

"I thought we were going right, and yet we came around in a circle. Trouble is, it is getting so confounded dark. Want to try going on again?"

"Yes, and we'll go more west than we have been going. We can't stand here and freeze."

They started forward once more, striking out in a new direction which seemed to both of them to be the right way. The wind was searching and they lowered their heads, both to keep their faces out of the cutting blast and to shelter their eyes from the driving snow. The sled, dragging along back of them, made slow progress through the mounting snow, and it caught frequently on the snags and bushes. From time to time they changed and took turns pulling it, but after a time Barry halted and came close to his chum, whom he could scarcely see in the gloom.

"I think we ought to leave the sled," he shouted.

Kent nodded, knocking snow off of his collar. "I have been thinking that, too," he returned. "We can't make any progress with it."

"We'll put it somewhere near a landmark, so that we will be able to find it again," Barry proposed, trying to look around. "After the storm we can come back and locate it."

"If we ever do come back alive," said Kent.

Barry slapped him on the back. "We'll come back, all right. We're only temporarily bewildered in a snowstorm. Let's find a place to leave the sled."

Kent took his flashlight off the hook on his belt and flashed it around. The light of it revealed falling flakes and an ever-increasing depth of snow on the ground. Advancing a few yards, they came to a tall shaft of rock and earth that formed a shelter from the driving power of the New England storm. It was with relief that they got out of the direct path of the wind.

"Here is as good a place as any," Barry proclaimed, pulling the sled in close to the foot of the small bluff. "We may have a hard time finding the spot, but at least we know the sled will be under an overhang of dirt and stone. This wouldn't be a bad place in which to spend the night, if we had to."

"I hate the thought of staying out in this cold all night," Kent shook his head.

"So do I. Seems like my skin is pinched hard. I wonder if we can't start a fire going here and eat something?"

Kent again flashed the light around. "It will be a hard job, but it will be worth trying. I think we can get some dry wood out of that log over there. As long as we have the sled with us, we ought to use the food on it."

"You're right. We haven't anything to make coffee in, and about the only food we can eat is the steak we bought. We can spear that on a stick and cook it. Let's try it."

Almost feeling their way, they began to chop into the wet log with the camp axes which they carried at their belts. The top wood was soft and pulpy, and even that which they hacked out of the heart of the log was not very dry. After the most tiresome efforts they succeeded in getting a pile of questionable wood together, and then came the task of setting it afire. Both of them huddled close to the pile and jealously guarded the tiny flame of the matches as they attempted to ignite the sticks and bits of wood. Six matches were soon wasted.

"This looks hopeless," Barry sighed. "Even the good store paper won't light."

Kent jumped up. "What dummies we are! This storm has us buffaloed! We have two long containers of kerosene oil on the sled!"

"Oh, good night!" exclaimed Barry, in disgust. "Of course we have! Douse this wood with it and then we won't have any trouble starting our fire."

Unscrewing the top of a container, Kent poured some of the oil on the massed-up wood and then replaced the oil can on the sled. This time they had no difficulty, and when the match flame touched the oil-soaked wood, the fire ran rapidly from chip to chip until all were blazing. The cold and hungry boys stooped low and held out grateful hands to the flame.

"Doesn't a fire feel good?" Kent exulted.

"Doesn't it?" his companion echoed. He straightened up and began to search under the sled canvas for the steak which they had purchased at Fox Point. "We'll have to get at our cooking right away, because when the oil burns off, this wood is going to be poor material, especially when we add more to it."

"You're right about that," Kent acknowledged. "I'll cut a couple of sharp sticks to cook the steak on." He took out his hunting knife and hacked at some bushes that showed dimly in the shadows from the fire. Before long he had procured two fine shafts, and then he proceeded to sharpen a point on each one. In the meantime Barry cut the steak in two and then cut it again.

"Maybe some of those things on the sled ought to go with us when we leave here," he observed, as he thrust the pointed stick through the steak. "We don't know how long we may be on the march, and we'll want food with us."

"Too bad we haven't got a knapsack along," Kent declared.

"It is, but we have some good pockets that will take a few things. Once this storm clears, we'll be able to see something. Unfortunately, we don't know when it will let up."

They became silent, holding the portions of steak over the blaze, and soon the meat was browning and the juice dripping into the fire. As Barry had said, the quality of the blaze soon became poor, and when fresh fuel was added it was uncertain and smoky. But they managed to eat their steak, and it went a long way toward giving them a better feeling.

"I missed salt and bread with it," Kent smiled, as they finished the steak. "But it certainly was good all by itself. Well, what shall we do?"

"I believe that we ought to go on. This fire doesn't amount to anything, and there is no use hanging around here all night. We don't want to use up our oil on the fire, and we would have to work all night to cut wood for it."

"Then let's tie the canvas down tight over the sled and cover it up with some branches so that no wandering animal can get into it," Kent proposed, and they spent some time in doing this. When this task had been attended to, they set out once more, heading into the dashing flakes once more.

"The twins will be badly worried," Barry said, as they stumbled along, making better time now that they were no longer held back by the burden of the sled.

"Yes, they will. I hope they won't come out and try to find us."

"I doubt that they will. They can see how bad the storm is and that they would be lost in no time at all. Boy, that flashlight of yours is a life-saver!"

There was no question that the flashlight was tremendously valuable. Kent used it sparingly and turned it on only at intervals, but it guided them on their journey. They kept on going and at last were ready to give up in despair, as they had passed no home and even the country did not look familiar to them. At last Barry halted and looked around.

"Flash your light up," he directed. "Where are we?"

Kent played the light around him, and they saw that they were in an old quarry. The rock walls gleamed in the faint light of the flash.

"A quarry!" Barry cried.

Kent played the light down toward the ground, and they saw a small shed. "There is shelter, if we need it," he began. At that moment the flashlight slipped out of his hand and fell into the snow. "Doggone it," he grumbled. "I dropped the light."

Both of them stooped to search for it and then paused as they heard a sound near them. Someone was approaching, and they felt a great relief as they realized it. Neither of them spoke, and a moment later a light flashed out, evidently from a flashlight. The beam rested on the shed, and the boys waited to see the face or form of the one who held it. But they were destined to be disappointed. A hand came into the center of light and turned the knob on the shed door. The hand was sheltered in a black glove, and that was all that they saw of the person who opened the door of the quarry shed. The light was instantly extinguished and the door slammed shut. They heard a key turn in the lock.

"Wonder who that was?" Kent asked. He had found the flashlight, and they both stood up and tried to see things more clearly.

"I don't know. Funny he didn't hear us or see our light."

"The wind is too loud for him to have heard us. Seems as though he should have seen our light. Going to ask for some help?"

"Of course. We don't know our way, and we need to have someone tell us. We'll knock on the door."

Approaching the small quarry shed, Barry knocked on the door, and they waited. The wind still blew strongly, and the flakes drifted down into the abandoned quarry. No answer came to their summons, and Barry tried again. They listened with growing impatience.

"It's a wonder he wouldn't open the door or at least call out," Kent growled.

Barry took Kent's flashlight and flashed the beam around. The shed was backed up against a dirt section of the quarry wall, and the windows were boarded up. It was impossible to look into the little shelter. He walked around on the far side and found that conditions there were the same. Then they once more stood before the door and listened.

Barry kicked the door. "Is anybody here?" he shouted. "We're two boys that have lost our way, and we want to ask directions."

The only answer was a profound stillness from the inside of the quarry shed. The boys looked at each other, and angry thoughts leaped into their minds. They had been adrift in the cold and storm so long that this lack of common humanity on the part of the man whom they had seen enter the shed aroused them.

"He's hiding in there and won't answer," Kent cried. "We ought to kick the door in!"

"I'd like to know what he's hiding for," Barry said. "He must have some reason for not wanting to talk to us."

CHAPTER XVII
The Black Shadow

Losing his temper for the moment, Kent launched two heavy kicks against the door of the quarry shed. The sound boomed out across the big cleared space, and the boys listened expectantly, hoping that this vigorous summons would bring results. But no answer came to them.

"Let's break in," Kent proposed. "We can't freeze to death out in the open, and besides that, I'd like to tell that man inside what I think of him. We can crash that door down."

For a moment Barry was swayed by the idea. It seemed to them as though they had been cold and lost for ages, and the prospect of warmth and shelter from the driving wind was alluring. But as he considered it, he shook his head.

"I don't think we ought to, Kent. For some reason that we don't know, whoever went into the shed is hiding. That shows he is up to no good. Such a person may have a gun on him, and if we break in, we may get shot."

"I suppose you're right, but I do want to have a few words with that fellow. No matter who he is or what he is up to, he could at least shout out directions. What are we going to do? Wait awhile until he comes sneaking out?"

"We could do that. We could hide and watch the place and then go into it when he comes out. But look here, isn't this quarry familiar to you? Isn't it the one we can see from the lodge?"

Kent looked around, impatiently brushing the snow from his collar. "I don't know. All quarries look the same, especially in a storm."

"I know it, but how many quarries are there near the lodge? Only one that I know of, and we can see that one from the place."

"If that is true," said Kent, thoughtfully, "we have just wandered around in a big circle and come around in back of the lodge instead of approaching it from the side. By golly, we may be almost home!"

"I wouldn't be surprised." Barry pointed through a gap formed by the quarry and the dark, snow-laden trees of the forest. "The lodge would be in that direction, wouldn't it?"

"I think so. Shall we hike that way?"

97

"Yes, let's go. No use standing around here."

"But suppose we're wrong? We ought to try and get back here and break into this little building. We might wander until we're exhausted, drop and then freeze. More than one hunter has done that, you know."

"If we find we're wrong, we'll try and make our way back here," Barry said. "But I just have a hunch that the lodge lies in that direction. We'll try it."

Spurred on by the faint hope that they might be somewhere near their camp, the boys hurried out of the bowl of the quarry and once more plunged into the woods. They found that their feet had become numb from standing, and they winced as they began their journey. The wind was still sharp, but the snowflakes had thinned out and the storm was obviously letting up. There had been considerable snow, however, and their feet sank deep into it as they traveled on.

"I believe that the storm is letting up," Barry said, as they tramped on, heads down and faces bent to escape the bite of the wind.

"That will be a help," Kent acknowledged. "But isn't this cold intense? I'd give something to be out of this wind and to get my feet warm. I don't want to kick a rock or a tree root, for fear of knocking a couple of toes off!"

"When we get up to the top of this slope, we may be able to see our way and figure out where we are," Barry consoled.

"We've had mighty bad luck," Kent said. "We haven't come across a single home, and there are some in these mountains, but our wanderings have taken us away from them."

"Yes, if we had run across a house, we could have put up for the night. We may do so yet. Well, in a few minutes we can see something."

Toiling on up the slope, they came at last to a break in the timber, and their anxious eyes scanned the dark landscape for any signs that might guide them. Then Barry pointed.

"I wonder if that is a light off there? It's pretty small and still some distance away. What do you think?"

"Looks like a light to me. We might as well go in that direction and see. It is as good as walking around blindly."

98

They set off at a faster pace, and soon there could be no doubt that a light of some kind was before them. The confirmation of their hope caused their spirits to rise rapidly.

"It is either our camp or some house," Barry said, as he walked on with a new vigor in his stride. "Whichever it is, it means warmth for us."

"I hope it is the camp, but if it isn't, a house will be all right," observed Kent. "Unless the people there are like the man who hid in the quarry shed."

"We won't find many like that, thank goodness," Barry remarked.

For a short distance they lost sight of the light as they crossed a low section of ground where many bushes grew, and then when they once more came out on high ground a joyous shout burst from Kent. "It is the lodge!" he shouted. "Hurrah, we're located at last. See the old cabin over there, beside it?"

"Yes, there is no doubt of it," agreed Barry, thankfully. "Boy, does that place look good to me! Before long we'll be hugging the fire!"

"We'll give it a big bear hug," Kent promised. "Gosh, I am glad to be back safely. Things looked black for us for a while."

"They certainly did," Barry agreed, soberly. "Too bad we didn't bring the sled on with us, but we just didn't know."

"It's all right," Kent assured him. "With this depth of snow on the ground it was hard to pull the sled, and we have made better time without it. I believe we can find our way back to the place where we left it."

"So do I. We've got to get Mac's sausage for him! To say nothing of our oil and the other things on the sled."

Their spirits were climbing with every step, and now that the cold adventure was about over with, they felt strength and confidence returning. With the knowledge that they would soon be reunited with the boys in the lodge, they were beginning to forget the suffering and anxiety of their wandering in the storm.

They approached the lodge from the timber that grew close to the back of it, and as they drew nearer, they heard three loud thumps.

"The boys must be nailing something on the walls," Barry remarked.

"I'm glad they left that lamp in the window," Kent observed. "It has been a life-saver for us."

"Here comes one of them around the house," Barry exclaimed. "I wonder what he is doing?"

The returning travelers were just on the point of leaving the shelter of the trees and crossing the open space to the lodge when the appearance of someone from the porch stopped them. A figure in black raced along the side of the lodge and crouched near the window where the lamp stood. At the same time the lamp was taken away and the boys in the woods saw Tim's face briefly through the window.

"Say, that's not Tim or Mac!" Barry cried, in a low tone, as they stood and looked at the black shadow stooping beneath the window. "The boys are in the house! Something is going on here!"

"Something funny, too," Kent quivered. "Want to tackle that fellow by the window?"

Before Barry could answer, the black shadow straightened up and ran to the back of the lodge, disappearing in the tool house. The man seemed to have a long overcoat on, and he was a weird sight as he fled with long, loping strides to the tool house. Barry grasped Kent's arm.

"Kent, that's the spook of this lodge!"

"Sure thing!" his companion breathed. "We've got to get him!"

"Listen," proposed Barry, rapidly. "You sprint for the lodge and get the twins. Bring the guns with you. I'm going to watch that tool house so that the man doesn't get out and give us the slip. Step to it!"

Kent needed no urging. He was a little too stiff to run well, but he did the best he knew how and covered the distance from the woods to the lodge in fairly good time. The porch creaked as he ran across it, and he threw open the front door without ceremony. Then he received a surprise as he came face to face with the twins.

They were standing in the cold hall, and Tim held the lamp, which Mac had just lighted. The poker was on the floor at Mac's feet, and they turned with startled faces as Kent dashed in at the door. Then Tim's face darkened with anger.

100

"Oh, it was you fellows, after all," he began, with some heat. But Kent interrupted him.

"It was like fun! There is a man hiding in the tool house. We saw him run around the lodge. Get the rifles and come on! Barry is watching the tool shed!"

The twins lost no time. Mac forgot about the poker and ran into the living room, returning with the rifles and his hat and Tim's.

"How about the lamp?" Tim asked, as he seized his hat.

"Leave it here," Kent returned, curtly. "I have my flashlight. Come on!"

They raced across the front porch and jumped into the snow, the twins shivering with cold as they came in contact with the outside air. Barry had moved in from the timber and was standing near the back porch. Mac tossed him his rifle, which he caught on the run. Tim had taken the poker, and Kent had his rifle. Mac alone was not armed, but Kent passed the flashlight to him.

"He's still in there," Barry told them, as they stopped outside the door. "I haven't taken my eyes off of the place since you left, and he hasn't come out. Turn on the light, whoever has it."

Mac pressed the button, and the beam of light showed the door. Barry wasted no time in summoning the one who was inside. With his rifle held forward he pushed the door of the tool house. Kent was close to him, and Tim brought up in the rear.

They were all excited and a trifle scared, but the general feeling was that the black shadow should be captured at once. Under Barry's push the door yielded slightly, and it was evident that it was not locked. He gave it a stronger push, and it rushed back against the wall with a crash. The light from the flash swept into the shed.

Their nerves were tense and eyes strained as they looked about the tool house. And it was Barry who voiced the conviction of all of them:

"He got away! There's no one in the place!"

CHAPTER XVIII
Down River

The mystery hunters were astonished and baffled as they gazed into the interior of the tool shed of the haunted lodge. No one was in the place. The garden tools hung in order, a large bale of hay stood back against the wall, but no human being was to be seen. Nor was there anywhere to hide. Mac turned the beam of the light upward. There was no loft, only some cross braces of wood that would not hide even a cat.

"But we saw him come in here," Kent protested, as they stood and looked around.

"And I never took my eyes off of the shed," Barry added. "I ran across from the woods and didn't even watch my footing because I wanted to keep my eyes on the place. I can't figure it out."

Tim pointed to a small window in the rear.

"Maybe he slipped through that."

Barry crossed the floor of the tool house and tried the window. It was not locked, and it lifted inward.

"Well, he might have, though I don't see why I shouldn't have seen it at the time. Looks as though that was his only way. Perhaps he heard or saw me running across to the back porch and he slipped out of the window as we were approaching the front. Too bad, but he is gone."

"I'm convinced that it was our spook, too," Mac said.

"Let's take a look around back and see if we can find any footprints," proposed Kent, and, going to the back of the tool shed, they looked around. But a mass of briar bushes grew close to the rear of the small building, and they were unable to find any clues.

"Nothing doing," Barry sighed. "He has given us the slip."

"Let's get inside," suggested Tim, who was feeling the cold intensely.

"Yes, you fellows aren't dressed for outdoors," nodded Kent. "And we are just about crazy to get in around the fire. We'll have to give this up as a bad job, for the time being anyway."

With some reluctance they left the vicinity of the tool house and made their way around to the front of the hunting lodge. The boys had left the front door open in their haste, and the hall was even colder than it had been. The twins led the way into the living room of the lodge.

"Welcome to Bluff Lodge!" Mac cried, taking the poker and beginning to stir the fire. Barry and Kent spread grateful hands toward the blaze.

"Coal on the fire!" Barry exclaimed. "Where did that come from?"

"There is a coal shed back of the kitchen," Tim explained. "Feels good, doesn't it?"

"Does it!" Kent and Barry ejaculated in chorus. "You don't know the half of it!"

"Been out in the woods in all this storm?" Mac asked.

Barry nodded. "Yes, we have been lost. Had to leave the sled and find our way. It was a great idea on the part of you fellows to put the lamp in the window."

"Have you had any supper?" Tim asked.

"Yes, we had plenty. Built a fire and cooked some steak," Kent told him. "But I'd surely appreciate a hot cup of coffee. How about you, Barry?"

"Yes, indeed," his chum agreed. He began to take off his outer clothes, shaking snow into the fireplace. "We've all got stories to swap. What was that man doing besides thumping on the side of the house?"

While the coffee was preparing they sat close to the fire and talked. The twins told their story first, and the two who had been lost listened with close attention. Then, while they all drank hot coffee, Barry and Kent related the events of the day.

They had put the lamp out, and the fire glowed red. A feeling of comfort and security settled over them, in spite of the lurking presence of the one who was seeking to annoy them. Although they were tired they had too much to discuss to want to go to bed at the moment.

"So you didn't bring home Mac's hog grindings," Tim grinned.

"We were lucky to bring ourselves home," Kent retorted. "But we are sure that we know where the sled is, and if the storm lets up tomorrow, we'll go get it."

Mac went to the window and looked out, shielding his eyes from the light of the fire. "I believe that the worst of it is over already," he declared.

"The flakes are coming down slowly." He turned back and sat down in a wicker chair. "We certainly are glad to see you back again."

"The sight of this lodge was certainly a most welcome one," grinned Barry. "We didn't care whether it was haunted or not!"

They talked for a time and then sought their beds. Kent and Barry were pleased at the change of quarters. They lugged in the mattresses from the beds in the cold bedrooms and placed them on the floor. Mac selected the wide sofa for his resting place, and when they had washed and were ready, they stretched out on the mattresses with various feelings of satisfaction.

"I never was so tired," Kent yawned.

"What about keeping guard?" Tim suggested. "Suppose that thumping, knocking idiot comes around again?"

"I won't hear his thumping or knocking," Barry predicted, with a grin.

"I won't, either," Kent said. "Looks like you Ford boys will have to do the chasing."

"I'm not going to chase him," Tim promised.

"We won't have to stand guard," was Mac's opinion. "I'm a pretty light sleeper, and maybe I'll wake up if anything goes wrong. We'll hope he doesn't come back again."

Little more was said, and the boys went to sleep, thoroughly exhausted. They had not slept well since coming to Lake Arrowtip, and there was no guarantee that they would not be disturbed before morning, but they went to sleep trusting that all would be well. This time good fortune was on their side, and they slept soundly until somewhat late in the morning. The mattresses were soft and comfortable, and the room was warm most of the night. Barry was the first to awaken, and when he had looked around and noted that his companions were still asleep, he lowered his head and slept for another half-hour.

Mac was the first to get up, and he looked at the clock. "Eight-thirty!" he whistled. "For the love of Mike, what hardy campers we are!" He reached over and took the poker and proceeded to beat on the side of the coal scuttle. "Wake up, the enemy is upon you!"

The others quickly woke up and looked around the room in some confusion. "You're the only enemy we have!" growled Kent.

"That's a sign that you are a great man," chuckled Mac. "All great men have enemies!"

For breakfast they finished up the pork and beans left from the previous night. Most of their provisions were on the sled, and as soon as they had set the lodge in order they prepared to set off for the woods to find the missing vehicle. It had stopped snowing sometime during the night, and the sun was struggling to come out of the gray clouds.

"I guess the spook didn't come back last night," Tim remarked, as they started out.

"If he did, I didn't hear him," Barry declared. "I slept like a log the whole night. Not even a dream disturbed me."

"I wasn't quite as lucky as that," Kent told them. "I kept dreaming over and over again that I was wandering around in circles. But I didn't hear anything, not even Mac's snores!"

"I don't snore," retorted Mac. "At least I've never heard myself!"

Barry and Kent were going by guesswork and at first were unable to find the place where they had left the sled, but just as they were becoming discouraged Kent pointed off to the left. "There's a small bluff, and it looks like it might be the place," he said.

"It was snowing so hard at the time that we couldn't be certain of anything," Barry said. "But that looks like the place. Yes, it is!"

They found the sled still buried under the tree limbs and bushes, but it was evident that some animal had been scratching around in an effort to get at it. "Probably a fox," was Tim's guess. Nothing had been disturbed, however, and they started back to the lodge with the sled. As they came out of the timber Mac pointed ahead of them.

"Somebody is standing close to the lodge," he said, in a low voice.

They saw a man standing near the front porch, looking around him as though in perplexity. He was evidently a woodsman, and he held something in his hand. Upon seeing the boys he hastened to meet them.

"Howdy-do," he greeted. "Which one of you boys is named Garrison?"

"I am," Barry informed him. The man held out a letter.

"Here's a letter to you. I passed through Fox Point this mornin', and I'm goin' down to the head of the lake, so the storekeeper asked me to take it."

"Thanks a lot," Barry acknowledged, noting that it was from his father.

"You're welcome, sure," the man replied, as he turned away.

"Stop and have some dinner with us," Kent called, but the man smiled and shook his head.

"Had mine already, thanks to you," he replied and was soon out of sight.

Barry read his letter while the others were preparing dinner, and his face was a study as he finished it. "No bad news, is there?" Kent asked.

Barry shook his head. "No, but my Dad says we had better come on home. School starts again Tuesday, and he thinks I ought to be home so as to get ready to study for the next term. When he wrote this, he hadn't received my letter, of course. I suppose we'll have to go back."

The others had stopped their preparations for the noon meal and had clustered around. "That means go home tomorrow," Mac pointed out.

Barry nodded. "Yes, it does. And I think we ought to get up early and make our trip all in the one day, instead of camping out overnight again."

"It can be done easily enough," Kent agreed. "Well, I didn't realize that our time was up so soon. We haven't solved our mystery, either."

"That's exactly what is bothering me," Barry declared. "We have been here long enough to have the ghost or prowler make raps and knocks, and then we have let him slip right out of our fingers. It won't be easy to tell that to Dad, though I feel sure that he'll understand that we did the best we could. But it is a big disappointment to me."

"We really should have had more time on the case," Tim said. "Maybe something will happen tonight and we can lay hands on the one we want."

"That's our only hope," Kent declared. "Something must happen tonight!"

They spent the afternoon at the lodge, and for supper Mac had his sausage. After supper they chatted and enjoyed their last evening in the hunting lodge. They arranged to take turns watching through the night, and Barry took the first session. While the others slept, he sat in a big chair back in the shadows, his eyes and ears alert. Mac followed him and then the others, but nothing amiss happened, and when daylight came, they were forced to realize that their last chance had passed.

"Nothing doing, we've failed," remarked Barry, somewhat bitterly.

As soon as they had had breakfast they set the lodge in order and then left it, making sure that everything was in its place. At the edge of the lake skates were strapped on, and they struck out briskly. Before the sun had risen very high they had entered the mouth of Buffalo and were going downriver at a good pace. It was evident that they would arrive in Cloverfield soon after dark. But the thought did not make them as happy as it should have. They were deeply disappointed at their failure.

"Maybe we can come back in the summer and camp there," Tim said, as they talked it over around the fire of their noon camp.

"The summer is a long way off," declared Barry gloomily. "I wish we had landed him this time. But I guess we lost our opportunity once and for all."

CHAPTER XIX
An Interview with a Client

As the boys had calculated, they reached Cloverfield well after dark. In discussing it at noontime, they agreed not to pause for an evening meal, but to push on and get home as soon as possible. Accordingly, they kept up a fast pace, and had it not been for frequent detours around snow-covered places and logs, they would have made it by early darkness. But as it was, they did well and saw the lights of their home city before them at 7:30 o'clock. By eight they had reached their homes, and Barry went in after a few final words with Kent. The light and warmth struck him pleasantly as he stepped in the door.

His mother and sister were in the kitchen washing and drying dishes, and his father was just coming up from the cellar, where he had been putting more coal on the furnace. They heard his footsteps along the hall and greeted him eagerly.

"We didn't know whether you would get in tonight or tomorrow," his mother said, as she kissed him.

"Did you have your supper?" Pearl asked. "I'll get you some if you didn't."

"I haven't had any, Pearl, and I'll tell Mac what a nice girl you are if you'll get me some," Barry answered, with a grin.

"Oh, get out!" Pearl retorted, her cheeks flushing. "If you keep on talking that way, I won't do anything for you!"

"I got your letter, son," Mr. Garrison told him. "So you moved into the lodge when you found that someone had been upstairs in the place. Have any luck? Did you see anything?"

"The only luck we had was bad luck," Barry replied, as he took off his coat and hat and hung his skates in the cellar-way. "We saw the spook and thought we had him bottled up, but he got away."

"What!" cried his father, in genuine astonishment. His mother looked on in surprise, and Pearl turned from the ice box to glance at him.

"Oh, Barry! What did he look like?"

109

"He looked just like a man, but we didn't see his face," her brother informed her, as he washed his hands. "I'll tell you all about it while I eat."

They were all so eager to hear his story that all three of them fell to waiting on him, and while he ate he told them the complete story of the black shadow who had made the thumps and knocks. His father listened with puckered brow and leaned forward on the kitchen table in his eagerness.

"I'm glad you and Kent weren't lost in that storm," his mother said, looking fondly at her clean-cut, vigorous son.

"My goodness, I would have been scared to death if I had seen that figure run along the side of the lodge!" Pearl declared.

"Barry, I think Mrs. Morganson ought to hear that story," Mr. Garrison remarked. "Feel like going over to her house tonight?"

"Of course, Dad, if you give me time to clean up a bit. I'm still dressed as a camper, you know."

"That won't bother Mrs. Morganson, but I agree that you ought at least to change your shirt. You do that as soon as you have finished, and I'll telephone her and ask if we may come over."

Barry nodded his agreement, and his father was soon talking to his client over the wire. In a few moments he came back, putting on his overcoat as he came.

"She says she'll be glad to see us," he said. "I'll get the car out, and we'll go over as soon as you are ready."

Barry rose from the table. "I'll be with you in a couple of shakes, Dad." He raced up the front stairs and before long was running down them again, with a clean shirt and his hair neatly combed. "Did Dad come in?" he asked his mother.

"No, he's out front, sitting in the car and waiting for you," she said. "He had faith in you when you said you'd only be a couple of shakes. He seemed to know what a shake is."

"Just two shakes of a lamb's tail, Mother. Is that all the time I took?"

"Yes, if the lambs shook them pretty slowly," Mrs. Garrison smiled.

110

Barry trotted down the walk and got into the car. "All right, Dad, here I am."

Mrs. Morganson lived on the other side of Cloverfield, and after driving several blocks Mr. Garrison brought the car to a stop in front of a fine old white house that stood back among some magnificent trees. As they opened the door to get out of the car, the front door of the big house opened, and a man came down the steps and approached them. As the lamplight revealed him, Mr. Garrison murmured his name.

"Brand Curry! I wonder.... Good-evening, Mr. Curry."

The rather chunky individual merely grunted and gave a short nod. He seemed out of humor and would have passed on, but Barry's father hailed him.

"Just a moment, Mr. Curry. Have you been in to see Mrs. Morganson about the Bluff Lodge proposition again?"

Curry swung around and faced him abruptly. "It is none of your business what I went to see Mrs. Morganson about, Mr. Garrison."

"I'm glad to hear that," the lawyer returned evenly. "If it was about that hunting lodge, it is my business. But if you weren't talking about that, it wasn't."

"I did go see Mrs. Morganson," the man admitted defiantly.

"Well, that's just what I thought, Mr. Curry. Why don't you come to me? I am her representative, and she is not to be bothered with the details. Why is it that you don't come to me?"

"Mr. Garrison, this is a free country, and I go where I like. I prefer to deal directly with Mrs. Morganson, that is all."

"Is it because you have no confidence in me, Mr. Curry?" Barry's father asked.

"I have my reasons, Mr. Garrison, and I will keep them to myself. Good night!"

Mr. Curry walked away with dignity, and Mr. Garrison shook his head in perplexity. "He's a hard man to deal with, and he never has been willing to talk over this particular deal with me. He didn't act very happy, did he?"

"No," Barry chuckled. "Maybe Mrs. Morganson told him to go and see you."

"We'll soon know," said Mr. Garrison, leading the way into the house. At his knock a servant let them in and showed them to a small private library where Mrs. Morganson was reading. She welcomed them with kindness, and they sat close to a grate fire as they talked.

"As I told you over the phone, Mrs. Morganson, my son has something of importance to tell you concerning Bluff Lodge," Mr. Garrison began. "He and three of his friends have been camping up on Arrowtip, and he learned some interesting things. The last two days that they were at the lake, they camped in the lodge itself."

Mrs. Morganson looked with interest at Barry, and her words were a distinct surprise. "I know that he and his friends have been camping in the lodge," she said. "Mr. Brand Curry has just been here to protest about it!"

CHAPTER XX
An Unexpected Event

Barry and his father exchanged glances. "To protest about it!" Mr. Garrison cried.

"Yes," the lady nodded. "He said that it lowered the value of the place to allow boys to camp there. He seemed quite annoyed about it."

"But how did he know that we were there?" Barry inquired.

"He said that someone who knew the place had been up there lately and saw the boys in the lodge. I asked him if they had done anything to hurt the place, and he said no, but that he thought it was wrong to allow boys to camp there."

"Well, he certainly has a nerve!" said Mr. Garrison. "That property doesn't belong to him, and he has nothing to say as to what shall be done with it."

"He wants it badly enough and as good as told me tonight that he will have it," Mrs. Morganson said.

"He is very discourteous about it all," frowned Barry's father. "I stopped him tonight and asked him why he does not come to me. He said it is a free country and he prefers to go to you directly."

Mrs. Morganson smiled a quiet smile. "Probably he thinks he can win me over, or even scare me. He is offering a very low price for the lodge, and I am not going to sell it at his figure. He knows the value of the property and could make a lot out of it, but I am not going to give my hunting lodge away. Now I'd like to hear Barry's story."

Barry told the owner of the hunting lodge what had happened while they had camped at Lake Arrowtip. "The only thing that we regret," he finished, "is the fact that we did not catch the man after we saw him go into the tool shed. We feel that if we could have had a few days longer, we would have learned the secret of the place."

"It is too bad that your short vacation came to an end when it did," acknowledged the lady. "But I think you did a fine bit of work as it is. Of course, I have believed all along that some human being is doing this unpleasantness, and not any ghostly being. The mystery is, who is doing it and why?"

"Do you believe that Mr. Brand Curry is doing it to lower the value of the lodge?" Barry asked slowly. Mrs. Morganson smiled at his father as she shook her head.

"Your father and I have wondered about that, but we do not believe that it is so," she said. "Mr. Curry is always here in town, and we cannot believe that the lodge is so dear to him that he keeps a sort of scare agent up there all the time. Just as soon as any party goes into the lodge, either in winter or summer, the annoyances begin. That would seem to indicate that whoever does it lives close by there all the time. We know that Mr. Curry is anxious to have the place, but so are three other business men who are offering better prices than Mr. Curry is."

"It is all mighty queer," Barry murmured. "Have you ever heard from your nephew since the letter came from Canada?"

"We have reason to believe that he is now in South America," Mrs. Morganson said. "I believe that he was taken away from my property because he had discovered something that certain parties do not want known."

"There was a Frenchman who disappeared at the same time," Barry pressed. "What of him? Was he married?"

"Yes, he was married, and his wife was also working at the lodge when her husband left. Nothing has ever been heard of them since that time."

For another half-hour they talked of the mystery, and then Barry and his father left. Nothing definite had been agreed to, though Mr. Garrison had expressed a desire to make a trip to Arrowtip himself and spend a night or two in the lodge alone. But Mrs. Morganson was not in favor of the idea.

"Let us wait until spring comes before we do anything else," she advised. "It is so cold and disagreeable now. I will not rent it to anyone from now on, and when the warm weather comes we can have some more private detectives put on the case. Let's not worry about it until later."

Barry and his father went home and talked over the situation at length, and it was agreed between them that when spring came they would go to the lake, together with the other boys, and have another opportunity to match wits with the disturbing element of the hunting lodge.

School was not to begin before Tuesday, and on Monday morning Barry stood at the general desk in the local post office, writing out a card. No one else was in the place at the time except the two clerks back of the windows. While Barry was busily engaged, the door opened and a schoolmate named Charlie Black came in. He was a short, energetic young fellow with glasses and shrewd, laughing eyes, a great favorite at the high school, where he led in debates and any form of public speaking.

"Hello, little fellow!" Barry greeted, using the name most frequently applied to young Mr. Black. "Looking for a letter from your girl friend?"

"Hello, mystery hunter! No, I'm going to buy some stamps." This having been taken care of, Charlie approached the desk and leaned on it.

"Say, I have some news that will knock your eye out!"

"Don't tell it to me then, because I need all my eyes. You ought not go around with such dangerous news," Barry grinned.

"Listen, Barry, this is great news. No fooling!"

"Well, why keep it to yourself? Let's have it!"

"No school for about ten days!"

"Why?"

"Big flue from the furnace burned out, and they have to have a special new one made. Hurrah, what luck!"

Barry shook his head in pretended disgust. "It is plain to see that you'll never amount to anything. Rejoicing because your opportunity to learn something is cut off. Your lack of wholesome ambition is pitiful!"

"Aw, listen, plaster saint, you're just as tickled as I am! The difference between us is that I'm honest! Say, I have some more news!"

"Good night, you've got enough of it in you to explode! Get it out quick. What else happened?"

"Nothing yet, but it is going to happen. As soon as I heard that there wasn't going to be any school for a while I thought it would be a dandy idea to have a straw ride. What do you say?"

"You mean hire a truck or wagon and a bunch of fellows and girls and go for a straw ride?"

"Sure. How else would you go on a straw ride?"

"Where will we go?"

"I don't know yet, but maybe to Potter's Mill or some place where we can build a fire and cook some supper and then we'll come on home. It's a lot of fun!"

"I know, I've been on one before, only it was in the summer and not in the winter. What's the matter with getting about three or four sleighs?"

"That's a good idea. Will you and Kent and the twins come along?"

"I guess so. When are you going to have it?"

"As soon as we can. I've talked to a few seniors about it, and they are willing. Well, I must get on. I'm chairman, and of course that means all the work falls on me. Funny name, chairman, isn't it?"

"Why?"

"Well, the chairman never gets a chance to sit down, and he doesn't need a chair! Ought to call him something else. I'm on my way."

"Wait a minute," Barry requested. "Who made you chairman?"

"Why, I did!" was the unblushing answer.

"That's what I thought, popgun! Go ahead and do your organizing and we'll be with you."

"All right, be careful crossing corners!" grinned the energetic Charlie Black as he fairly dashed out of the post office.

Barry followed more slowly, and as he strolled along the street his mind was busy with the contemplated straw ride and the mystery at Lake Arrowtip. At last he came to a stop, and his face brightened up.

"Of course!" he murmured. "Why not?"

Abruptly changing his course, he turned down a side street and was soon going up the walk to the home of Mrs. Morganson. He was readily admitted, and the lady received him in the parlor. Barry rapidly told her about the plans for the straw ride.

116

"What I want to ask you in particular, Mrs. Morganson, is this: may we ride up to the lodge and have our gathering there? I will personally guarantee that we will treat the place well, and it would not suffer any from our visit, and Coach Jordan and Mrs. Jordan will be with us, I'm sure. I think it would be a splendid place for us to have supper, and we could spend the night there."

"I am not in the least afraid that you would damage the lodge," Mrs. Morganson smiled. "Are you sure Coach and Mrs. Jordan will go with you?"

"Yes, ma'am, Coach Jordan and his wife always go with us, and I guess they will this time."

"Certainly, you may use the lodge if they do," Mrs. Morganson granted. "I'm just hoping you won't have any trouble with that unknown person that you saw the last time you were there."

"I hardly think we will," Barry said. "But if we do, Kent and the twins and I will be on the lookout, and perhaps we can learn something more about him."

A few minutes later Barry was on his way home, his mind busy with new thoughts and ideas. He was in a hurry to hunt up his chums and tell them of the latest events.

"This may be the very chance we have been looking for," he reflected, as he walked briskly along. "The man always starts something when a crowd gathers in the lodge, and we'll be there all night, if the bunch will agree to go to Lake Arrowtip. The four of us will be on the lookout for any such visit. I hope this will all work out as I want it to!"

CHAPTER XXI
The Straw Ride

After dinner that day Barry hunted up Kent and the twins and told them what he had in mind. They fell in readily with his plan and were enthusiastic regarding the delay in the opening of school.

"Too bad we didn't know that before we came home," Tim remarked. "We could have stayed on, and perhaps we would have run down the evil spirit of the lodge."

"Yes, that's so," Barry agreed. "But this is the next best thing. As a matter of fact, it may work out better. Every time that a crowd goes to the lodge, something happens, and we may make the spook play right into our hands."

"We're taking quite a chance," Kent shook his head. "I'm just wondering if the prowler comes out on the first night or if he waits for the second or third. We may not be troubled in any way."

"I know it is a long chance," Barry agreed. "But we won't lose anything if nothing happens."

"You say we ought to stay overnight," Mac spoke up. "Will the bunch do it? They may not want to go to Bluff Lodge in the first place."

"I'm going to see Charlie Black and try and make him enthusiastic," Barry smiled. "Then he'll get the others in the same frame of mind. I think we can work it."

His chums having agreed to the program, Barry went to the home of the dashing Charlie, whom he found in his den. The popular high-school debater was practising on a cornet when Barry entered the room.

"Hi!" greeted the cornetist, hastily lowering the shining instrument. "Come in! But as the sign over the doorway to the lower regions says, 'Abandon hope, all ye that enter here.'"

"I've abandoned all hope of hearing any real music," Barry grinned. "What are you trying to blow that thing for?"

"Music," was the brisk answer.

"You're pretty good at chin music," Barry replied. "I don't see why you want to blow a horn. But that is neither here nor there. I came to see you about our straw ride."

The cornet was tossed with unerring aim into a waste basket, where a pile of crumpled paper broke its fall. Charlie spun fully around in his chair.

"Listen! Fifteen of us are going, counting you and Kent and the Ford boys. There may be others, too. I'll see Coach and Mrs. Jordan tonight and see if they'll go along. How's that for progress?"

"Wonderful!" Barry admitted. "You're a great organizer, Charlie. Where are we going on this ride?"

"I still have Potter's Mill in mind. What do you think?—Oh, that's my dog. I call him Castor Oil!"

A large, flop-eared animal had come bounding into the den and jumped up on the leather couch where Barry was sitting. Before the boy could move, the dog had shot out a big red tongue and licked his face. Barry ducked and hastily brushed his hand over his cheek.

"Get down, Castor!" commanded Charlie, sternly, and the dog obeyed in a clumsy manner.

"What do you call him Castor Oil for?" Barry demanded.

"Because he is a big nuisance, follows me around and jumps on people. He's about as welcome as Castor Oil. I don't like to take him places. One day I was thinking up a name for him, and at the same time I was thinking that I didn't like to take him around with me. I tried to think of something else I don't like to take, and then the name just came by itself, somehow. Good name, eh?"

"Well, about the kind of name I'd expect you to give," grunted Barry. "But to get back to business, how about taking our party up to Bluff Lodge, on Lake Arrowtip? It is a dandy place, and we could stay all night. I got permission from Mrs. Morganson to use the lodge, if we want to."

"Humph! That's the haunted house, isn't it?"

"Well, the four of us camped in it a few days, and there is nothing the matter with us," Barry replied.

120

"That sounds like a good place to go," Charlie nodded, gently pulling the big ears of the dog with the questionable name. "What kind of a looking place is it?"

Barry described the lodge to him, and Charlie was enthusiastic. "Say, that will be a dandy place. Fireplaces and stoves and bedrooms and all. But we'd have to stay overnight, wouldn't we?"

"Yes, but we wouldn't mind that. Coach and Mrs. Jordan will be along, and there is plenty of room for us all. We can take enough for our supper and breakfast the following morning. How are you going to go?"

"In sleighs," Charlie returned. "It is an easy matter to get hold of sleighs. Of course, it isn't much of a straw ride when you take it in a sleigh. I've always thought of a straw or a hay ride as one where you go in a truck or a big wagon, with straw on the bottom."

"It doesn't make any difference," said Barry. "As far as that goes, we can put straw on the bottom of the sleighs. So you agree to the lodge proposition?"

"Sure thing! You ask all of them you see if they'll stay overnight, and I'll do the same. We'll make this a dandy outing. Say, want to hear a little music on my new cornet?"

"I don't care. My nerves are in pretty good order today!"

"Castor Oil's aren't," replied Charlie, as he took the instrument from the waste basket. "He howls every time I go at it."

After leaving Charlie Black's house Barry started home, intending to stop and see some of the boys who were going on the ride. As he came to a certain corner he heard the noise of an oncoming car, and as it was traveling at a fast pace, he paused on the curbing and let it rush past him. Glancing at the driver, he saw that it was Carter Wolf and one companion. They looked at him, but nothing was said, and the car passed on.

"So he is back from Rake Island," Barry reflected, as he went on.

That night at the supper table Pearl spoke about the contemplated trip. "I hear that we are going to stay overnight at Bluff Lodge, Barry. Did you plan that?"

"Yes," her brother nodded. "I didn't know that anyone except seniors were going."

"Just a few," Pearl answered. "I'm one of the lucky ones. I hope we don't see that black shadow or anything!"

"What is the idea of going up there, son?" Mr. Garrison asked.

"Two reasons, Dad," his son replied. "One is that the place is ideal for an overnight trip, and another is that we hope to draw the man out and perhaps get a chance to nail him. The twins and Kent and I will be on the lookout." He turned to his sister. "Pearl, please don't tell anyone about that black shadow or anything else. We want the whole thing kept absolutely quiet so that we can do something if we get the opportunity."

"I won't breathe a word, Barry, and I'll even try not to look scared," his sister promised.

"That's a big job for you boys." Mr. Garrison shook his head, doubtfully.

"I'm afraid you'll get hurt," his mother worried.

"I don't think so," was Barry's reply. "After all, nothing may happen. No one may come around. Besides that, Coach Jordan will be with us, and so will a number of the other fellows, so we ought not to have any difficulty."

Plans for the straw ride went forward in a satisfactory manner. Charlie Black took it upon himself to see everyone who could possibly go from the upper class, and in the end sixteen of the young people of Cloverfield High School consented to go and spend a night at Bluff Lodge. Of these sixteen, nine were girls and seven of them boys. The other two members of the sleigh party were the popular football coach and his wife, both of whom were young and in sympathy with the fun of the young people. It had been agreed that each one was to bring a certain item of the provisions to be used on the trip, and at last everything was in readiness.

On the night before they were to start, the four chums attended a motion-picture show, and when they came out they were surprised to see that it was snowing. They halted outside the bulk of the crowd and waited for Charlie to join them. They had seen him wave from the steps of the theater.

"The little chairman wants us," Kent remarked. "Let's see what he has in mind now."

"This snow will make our trip a pretty one, if it doesn't get too deep," Barry said, as they waited.

"It won't turn into a blizzard," Tim felt sure.

"What is all that arm-waving about?" Mac asked Charlie as he joined the group.

Charlie looked all around them in a mysterious way. "Have you fellows heard anything?" he asked.

"I've heard a whole lot of things, but maybe not what you mean," smiled Barry. "What's up?"

"Why, I heard that Carter Wolf and his crowd are going to try and break into our party, or break it up, or something. You know, there has been a lot of talking about our trip, and he heard it. He says he and some friends were shot at one night near that lodge, and that you fellows know very well that it is haunted."

"Just the same, we're not afraid to go up there," Kent replied. "Somebody did shoot at him near the lodge, but it wasn't us. I hope he doesn't spoil our party by scaring any of the fellows or girls."

"It won't scare them," Charlie cried. "They'll only want to go all the more. But we had better keep our eyes open for any monkey business from Wolf and some of his bunch."

"We will," Barry promised.

On the following day the straw-ride party started for Bluff Lodge. The sleighs all came together at Kent's house, and after they were all in their places, the procession started. In the foremost sled sat the chairman, and beside him, between Charlie and Barry, Castor Oil reared his big head.

"Couldn't keep him at home," Charlie explained. "I didn't want to take him."

It was a fairly long journey to the lodge, and so they started at noontime. By road it was much shorter than by going up the river. It was a clear, cold day, and they enjoyed the swift motion of the sleighs.

Talk and laughter ran high, and they called jokingly from sled to sled. It was late in the afternoon and dusk was just spreading across the lake country when they emerged from the timber and came in sight of the lodge building.

"Hurrah, we're here!" shouted Charlie, thumping Castor Oil, who barked in protest.

"So that is the haunted lodge?" a girl in the second sled cried. "I wonder if we'll see the ghost!"

CHAPTER XXII
Barry's Great Discovery

Barry jumped from the sled and took out the keys while the others were dismounting from the sleighs. Tim and Mac lifted a large oil can from the vehicle they had come in. The others stood in the snow and stamped their feet, glad to move about once more after sitting so long. Coach Jordan helped some of the boys tie the horses to the back-porch rail.

The sun had gone down in an angry red haze, and the darkness was spreading rapidly, accompanied by a cold that nipped and penetrated them. Although they knew that the lodge would be cold, the visitors were glad to follow Barry and the twins inside. Kent made a quick trip around the big log building to see if everything was all right, and he returned satisfied.

The twins lighted the lamps that were already in the big living room, and in the meantime Barry collected some wood, soaked it with oil, and touched the flame of a match to it. After the flames were leaping up the chimney he got some coal and put it on the burning wood. The room began to get warm slowly.

The girls and boys roamed around admiring the place, and at last they began to take off coats and hats as the room warmed up. From the living room Kent and Barry moved into the two bedrooms and lighted fires in them, so that they would be able to stay there all night without discomfort. Soon the grates in those rooms were glowing and the lodge had become comfortable. They decided to do their cooking in the kitchen, and accordingly a fire was kindled in the big range there. This was something more of a task because the stove was rusty and clogged with ashes and tin cans, left by some careless and untidy campers. The boys cleaned the stove out, and after this was done, the fire burned well.

Some of them favored using the dining room, but the majority vote was that they eat in the living room, by the light and warmth of the large grate there. All of them were hungry, and so the girls took charge of the supper preparation under the expert leadership of Mrs. Jordan. The boys sat in the living room with the coach and chatted about winter sports. In a very short time the delightful smell of things cooking reached them. The coach smiled as he heard the murmurs of appreciation.

"That's a tempting smell, boys," he said. "This Lake Arrowtip air is a great hunger-producing tonic!"

"We found it that way," Tim grinned.

Charlie was seldom able to sit still long at a time, and he bounded off to the kitchen, followed by the faithful Castor Oil. Before long he was back, rigged out in an apron and a paper hat, obviously in the capacity of a waiter. Disregarding the jokes of the boys, he began to set things in order for supper.

It seemed to the hungry boys that the meal was a long time coming, but the girls declared with spirit that it hadn't taken much time except to those who sat around waiting for it. The time finally came when they were all sitting close to the fire eating steak and potatoes, talking and enjoying themselves. All lamps had been put out, and only the red glow of the fire illuminated the room. But by this time the fire was a solid mass of glowing coals, and a sufficient light was rendered for all. Their shadows clustered on the wall back of them.

"And you four boys camped here for a few days, just like this?" a senior girl asked the four chums. "Wasn't it delightful?"

"We enjoyed it," Kent nodded. "We weren't here all the time, though. At first we camped over in that smaller cabin that you could see as we drove up."

"What made you leave it?" Mrs. Jordan asked.

This was getting close to things that the boys did not want to reveal, but before Kent could answer, Barry broke in. "That little cabin was cold, and the floor was hard to sleep on," he said. "Then one night a limb dropped on the roof and scared us quite a bit, so we decided to move in here. Tim and Mac did the moving, and Kent and I got lost in a storm that day."

"But what about all the ghost stories we hear?" another girl asked. "Is there a ghost around?"

"Pretty cold for a ghost," Barry smiled. "We've been here two hours or more and haven't heard anything yet."

126

"I hope we don't!" said another girl, looking around the room uneasily.

"It will be all right," Charlie Black assured her. "We'll let Castor Oil loose all night and he'll sic the ghost. He's a fine sic-er!"

"The spook will run if he ever finds out the dog's name!" said Mac, amid a general laugh.

"Coach, how about telling us a good ghost story tonight?" Bill Jefferson asked. "The atmosphere is just right."

"The atmosphere is all right," the athletic instructor smiled. "But I'm afraid of some nerves around here. I know a ghost story wouldn't bother the boys, but I don't want to upset the girls."

But the girls themselves begged him to tell at least one after the meal was over, and at length he agreed to do so. Coach Jordan was a good story teller, and many times he had spun some lively yarns while on overnight hikes with the boys of Cloverfield. He excelled in creepy mystery stories, and the young people looked forward with eager anticipation to a good one after supper.

"How about some boy volunteers to dry dishes?" Pearl asked, as they got up to carry plates back to the kitchen. "We did all the work of preparing supper. I know that most of you boys camp out, so you must know how to wash and dry dishes!"

"How about letting Castor Oil lick all the plates and then drying them over the stove?" Charlie shouted, but an indignant chorus of voices answered him, and he went off chuckling.

"All right, the men will take charge of the kitchen from now on," cried Coach Jordan. "No ladies allowed out there except to bring your plates."

"That's the spirit!" commended Ruth Carrier, the leader among the high-school girls. "We'll start to toast some marshmallows for you."

"Agreeable all around," Kent nodded, and the boys took over the kitchen work, while the girls went back to the living room to toast the marshmallows.

Mr. Jordan and Kent did the washing, and the other boys dried the dishes. After a time they looked around for a pail to put scraps in, but there was none in the kitchen. Barry seized a lantern.

"I think I remember seeing one in the tool house," he said, as he opened the back door. "I'll be right back."

The horses tied to the rail of the porch moved restlessly as he passed by them on his way across the board platform. Fodder had been brought for them, and as soon as the dishes were dried the boys planned to move the horses to a big shed back of the lodge which served as a combination barn and garage. Barry arrived at the tool house and went inside, peering around in the feeble light from the lamp. At the far end of the place he saw a tin can.

"There it is. I thought I remembered seeing it in here. This is just— — Ouch!"

He had tripped on something, and he flashed the light down to see what it was. He was close beside the bale of hay that stood there, and as he examined the floor he saw that it was slightly raised. This interested him, and he put his hand down and pulled the raised boards toward him. To his surprise several of them came up a few inches.

"What the dickens is this? Why——"

With a single motion of his arm he pushed the bale of hay aside and stared at the floor. A long trapdoor was revealed, and with trembling fingers he raised it, looking down into a deep well of darkness. A pair of wooden stairs ran down to the floor of a passage.

"An underground passage!" Barry breathed. "Now I'm beginning to see a few things!"

For several seconds he stood staring down into the tunnel, remembering how the black shadow had disappeared from the interior of the shed. Many conflicting thoughts crowded his mind, and his impulse was to go down and explore the passageway. But the severe cold made him think better of it, and, closing the trap and replacing the hay, he picked up the tin container he had come to get and went back to the lodge.

"I'll get my hat and coat on and get some of the boys to go with me," he thought, as he opened the kitchen door and went in.

Coach Jordan and his helpers were nearly finished. Barry left the can and went into the living room, picking up his coat and hat. Kent and the twins were not around at the time, and so Barry slipped out of

128

the front door alone. His chums were in the bedroom attending to the fire there.

"I'll just take a peek along that corridor myself," he decided, feeling in his pocket for his flashlight and noting with satisfaction that it was there. "Then maybe I'll take the whole crowd for a tour of it, providing it is safe to do so!"

Arriving once more in the tool house, he moved the bale of hay aside and raised the trapdoor, listening keenly before making a descent into the newly found passage. No sound came to him as he stood in perfect silence, and at last, thinking that it was safe to proceed, he turned on the beam of his light and carefully walked down the steps. There were seven steps, and when he reached the bottom he turned the light down the tunnel. He had closed the door of the opening and now stood alone under the earth.

The passage was long and sloped away farther than the shaft of light would reveal. With a rapidly beating heart he began to advance, walking slowly and quietly, his eyes alert and his nerves drawn tight. The thought came to him that he was drawing farther and farther away from his companions and that he ought to go back and get some of them, but the impulse to go on was too strong, and he kept advancing.

The tunnel was well made. He was able to walk upright and had to bend low only at one place where a tree root broke through and crossed the underground way. It was a dry place and not very cold. The sides of the tunnel had been carefully cut, and it seemed to him that it had been built for some definite purpose.

"But what can it be for?" he wondered. "Does Mrs. Morganson know that it is here? Maybe I'll know more about it all when I get to the end."

The end was near. He could see some boards before him, and a few moments later he stopped, playing the beam of the light against the boards that closed the tunnel. They seemed to be fairly new ones, and they simply fitted into the soil. He put out his hand to push against them and then thought better of it, pausing to listen once more, his flashlight out. The blackness seemed to crush in on him.

129

"No telling what is on the other side of that boarding. If I can't push it open, I'll go back and get the others."

No sound came to him, and so he again turned on the light and then pushed against the partition. To his astonishment it turned outward like a door, and his light showed him the interior of a small shed. Stepping through and closing the boards after him, he was surprised to see that it was on hinges and formed part of the wall of the small building in which he found himself. There were two windows and a door to the place, but otherwise the interior was perfectly bare. A conviction came to him.

"By George, this is the quarry shed where Kent and I saw the man with the black gloves go in! No wonder no one answered our knocks and kicks. The man had gone up the tunnel to the lodge, and when we got over that way, we saw him run into the tool house! I'm learning so much that it makes me dizzy!"

He opened the door of the quarry shed and stepped out. The wind, coming in from a break in the rock wall, had swept the snow away from the door, and the ground was hard and the snow at that particular place hard-packed. He closed the door and looked around. It was much the same as it had been the night he and Kent had stood there demanding shelter, except that the snow was not driving. He wondered where the black shadow came from, and he began to wander toward the far end of the quarry. For a while he did not use his light, and it was not until he was at the very base of the quarry wall that he flashed the light around. There was nothing to be seen.

"No house or anything down at this end," he reflected, turning. "I'd better go the other way."

Then his eyes fell on a figure crossing the bowl of the quarry, and instinctively he crouched down. It was the same black-clothed figure that they had seen once before, and the man went boldly into the quarry shed. Barry watched him with wildly beating heart.

"There he goes now!" he breathed. "On his way to the lodge to start something, I'll bet! And as sure as I'm a foot high, he'll discover that someone has been in his tunnel! Then what will happen?"

CHAPTER XXIII
The Raiders

The boys who remained in the kitchen helping Coach Jordan with the dishes were not long in finishing the job. Kent and the coach did the washing, and as fast as they turned out the dripping, steaming plates, the other boys snatched them up and dried them. There was a lot of good-natured fun about it all, and it was plainly to be seen that the boys from Cloverfield were enjoying the whole trip.

Coach Jordan kept them interested by his description of his travels and experiences, and at the time that Barry left the room on his way to the tool house he was telling of the days when he was a member of the great Fordson camp in the mountains of Kentucky. His account of the road-building and forest-ranging in the dense timber of the Southern upland was of great interest to the boys, and they laughed heartily at some of the rough experiences that he had encountered while staying in mountain log cabins and having to get up at three o'clock and shave with well water on frosty mornings. He told them of the great salt kettles rusting away in the mud of the little town that was at the time the shipping point for the Ford lumber and coal, a town which had at one time supplied all of the blue-grass state with salt. The boys listened with great attention.

"What's the difference between those mountains and these?" Tom Bailey asked.

"These mountains are pretty well known," the coach replied. "The people in them have been in contact with civilization for a long time, and tourist and the summer camper have come into them frequently. But in the Kentucky mountains we find an arrested civilization, and by that I mean that people poured into its hollows and gaps and then progress jumped clear over them and kept going west, while the mountaineer remained the same as he had been in the time of the Revolution. I have frequently seen old mountain women working the old-time spinning wheel, and many of them smoke a pipe all the time."

Kent had finished his work, and after drying his hands he went into the nearest bedroom to see how the fire was. Finding that it needed coal, he seized a bucket and flashlight and went out to get some. When he returned he met the twins in the hall.

"Here you are," Mac exclaimed. "We were wondering what had become of you."

"Just lugging in some coal," Kent explained. He entered the bedroom and began to fix the fire. "What are the girls doing?"

"They have toasted some marshmallows that melt right in your mouth," Tim replied.

"That's where you want 'em to melt. Sounds like you have had some."

"We did," Mac admitted. "Now that the dishes are done, we can all have some."

"Where is Barry?" Tim asked.

"I don't know," Kent answered, straightening up. "The last I saw of him, he had gone out to the tool house to get a pail. I suppose he is in the kitchen now."

"I wonder if anything will happen tonight," Mac said, in a low tone.

"I don't know, but we are going to keep our ears and eyes open," Kent told him. "If anything does happen, we want to be on the job. Well, let's get back in the living room."

They found all the young people gathered around the fire, and Coach Jordan and Bill Jefferson were taking off their hats and coats. "We put the horses in the barn," the coach explained. Then he rubbed his hands and held them close to the fire. "After being out there, this heat feels good."

Kent and the twins looked around the room. "Anybody seen Barry?" Kent asked.

Everyone looked around, and then one by one they shook their heads. "He brought that pail in and then left the kitchen," Charlie announced.

"He came in here and took his hat and coat," one of the girls remarked. "Then he went out into that hall toward the front door."

The twins exchanged troubled glances, and Kent glanced involuntarily at Pearl, who looked suddenly alarmed. "Too bad Pearl knows anything about this place," Kent thought. But he spoke

132

carelessly: "Oh, well, he'll be right back. Let's have some of those marshmallows. What happened to those black ones?

"Fell in the fire," Jennie Morrison explained. "But they'll taste just as good as the others. They are just like some people, rough outside and sweet inside!"

"Jennie is becoming quite a philosopher," laughed Mrs. Jordan. "Tell us some more!"

The girl laughed. "I can toast marshmallows better than I can give you philosophy," she said.

The talking went on in a good-natured way, but not all of them were joining in it. The three mystery hunters were quiet, and Pearl frequently looked at Mac, and she was plainly uneasy. Finally Mac leaned over to Tim.

"Listen, I don't like the looks of things," he whispered. "Barry has been gone a long time. Suppose you go into the kitchen and look around. If you don't see anything, I'll go out on the front porch."

"What excuse will I give for going out?" Tim asked.

"You don't need—well, there isn't any water in here, and there is some in the kitchen. Go ahead."

Tim nodded and got up from the footstool upon which he had been sitting. "These marshmallows are powerful sweet," he smiled. "I'm going to get a pitcher of water and some glasses."

"That's a good idea," the coach approved.

Tim took his flashlight and hurried to the kitchen. They had brought some large containers of drinking water with them, and just now this afforded him a convenient excuse for leaving. But as soon as he arrived in the kitchen he put out the light and walked across the room to the back door. He turned the key and looked out.

All was quiet, and no one was around. He walked out on the porch and looked around the open clearing. The night was fairly dark, but because of the bright blanket of snow he was able to make out near-by objects. Barry was nowhere to be seen. Tim returned to the house, locked the kitchen door, and proceeded to pour some water in a pitcher by the light of his flash. When he had obtained some glasses he went back to the living room.

Mrs. Jordan was reciting a humorous poem, and most of them paid little or no attention to Tim as he came back. But Pearl scanned his averted face anxiously and saw at once that he had not found her brother. Mac and Kent read the same answer.

Nothing was said, and at last Mac began to work his way toward the hall door. Tim had passed him the flashlight, and with this in his back pocket he gradually moved over to the door that led into the front room. While the others were busy laughing at a joke that Charlie had told, Mac slipped out of the door. Few of them saw him go, and no one asked any questions.

As soon as he got into the big square hall Mac turned on the beam of the light and hastily played it all around the box-like place. Barry was not there, and for a moment Mac trained the light on the stairs leading to the loft. He wondered if his chum had gone up there, but at last he shook his head. The popular leader of Cloverfield High School had put on his hat and coat, and that clearly indicated that he had gone out-of-doors. For a moment Mac hesitated. He was not prepared to go out into the snow, and to go back and get his outer clothing would excite suspicion at once.

"And yet," he reflected, "the bunch is soon going to know that Barry has disappeared. If he doesn't get back soon, we'll have to go and look for him. We can't fool them much longer. Pearl is getting more and more uneasy every minute. Hang it all, maybe we're wasting valuable time. I'll look outside, and if I don't see him, I'm going back and get my hat and coat and go out and hunt for him."

He stepped out onto the front porch and walked to the edge, looking around toward the back of the lodge. No one was in sight, and then he glanced out over the lake, dim in the light of the stars and the white border of the dark timbered sides. At once his eyes narrowed as he saw signs of movement on the ice sheet of the lake. Something bulky and black shot out onto the ice, and two figures leaped from it and began to push it ahead of them. As Mac stared without comprehension, another bulky object shot out from the bank onto the ice. The Ford boy gasped and clenched his fists.

"Our sleighs! Somebody is shoving them out onto the lake! Of all the——"

A voice, low-pitched and yet penetrating, reached him, coming in from the lake. "Don't send the other one down until I tell you! I want to get this one out of the way first!"

A great light dawned upon Mac. "Carter Wolf and his gang!" he breathed, as he turned and raced softly back to the front door. "Running off with our sleighs! Going to hide them so we'll have to hike home! We've got to put a stop to that!"

Throwing all caution to the winds, the twin rushed through the hall and flung himself into the living room, startling them all and very nearly knocking one girl over. His staring eyes and excited manner alarmed them all and caused particular apprehension on the part of those who knew anything about the history of Bluff Lodge.

"Listen!" he said, before anyone could speak. "Somebody is pushing our sleighs out on the ice and taking them off to hide them. I'm sure it is Carter Wolf and his bunch! If we don't want to walk home tomorrow, we'd better get out there in a big hurry!"

A medley of cries of surprise and indignation came in answer to his rapid announcement, and everyone sprang up in consternation. Coach Jordan seized his coat and hat.

"Come on, boys," he cried. "We'll have something to say about this!" He turned to his wife. "You take care of the girls, Dorothy. Better not go out!"

The boys were ready, and like a pack of hornets they dashed out of the front door on the heels of Coach Jordan. Kent sprinted in the lead because he knew the country better, and he led them across the clearing toward the Bronson cabin. They had left the sleds in front of that building when they had tied the horses to the back-porch rail.

All of the sleighs were gone, and Mac led them down the slope toward where he had seen the sleighs slide out on the ice. They expected to find the vehicles scattered and the raiders gone. But to their astonishment they heard voices and saw a dark mass at the edge of the lake shore.

"Keep his head above water!" a voice cried out. "We'll try to pull this sleigh out. Keep a stiff upper lip, Carter!"

"Get—get me out!" a voice gasped. "I told you not to let that sleigh go until I told you to!"

By this time the boys and the coach had arrived on the spot, and Mac's flashlight showed the scene before them. One of the sleighs was turned sideways, and another had run into it and was partly sunk under the ice. Caught under a runner, and immersed in water to his chin, was Carter Wolf. The sleigh had broken the ice, and he had gone in with a splash. The sleigh runner had pushed in on top of him and was pressing against his chest, while his five friends worked frantically to hold his head above water and at the same time to pull the winter conveyance back out of the break in the ice.

"What happened here?" the coach cried, as they took in the scene.

"These f-f-fellows let a sleigh come down the hill b-be-before I had moved the other one out of the way," Wolf answered, with chattering teeth. "The ice was thin here and——" In his effort to talk he slipped slightly and swallowed some icy water.

"Keep perfectly still," the athletic coach commanded. "We'll get you out." He lay down flat on the ice and passed his gloved hands under Wolf's armpits, feeling the shock of the cold water. It was a position of extreme peril for Coach Jordan if the ice broke away, but he did not allow his mind to dwell on the thought. "Now, the rest of you boys draw that sleigh up out of the hole."

The girls had followed and now stood on the shore, silent except for a few low-voiced exclamations, their faces white as they saw what had happened. Mac sprang up the bank and pressed his flashlight into Mrs. Jordan's hand.

"Keep this trained on us, please," he requested, and then he was back with the others, lending a hand.

The sleigh was a big one and had considerable weight to it, but by their united efforts they managed to move it backward. Coach Jordan had considered using some of the horses, but time was pressing, and he knew that Wolf must be rescued as soon as possible. The boys

136

pulled and tugged steadily, and the sleigh was finally drawn up on the bank and off of the ice.

"Now, two of you come here!" the coach called. "Only two, and come around in a circle back of me so as not to put too great a strain on the ice!"

Two of Wolf's companions quickly and carefully circled around the gaping hole and made their way to the coach. His friends were quiet and obviously frightened by the recent events. Also, they were quite willing to help, and although somewhat afraid to trust the ice, they knelt beside the athletic instructor and helped him lift Carter Wolf out of the icy waters of Lake Arrowtip.

"Two of you boys race to the lodge and get some blankets," Jordan directed.

Tim started on the jump. "Come on, Mac," he cried, and his brother joined him at once.

Kent watched them run up the slope toward the lodge and then turned to look on as Coach Jordan and Wolf's two friends guided him as he stumbled toward the shore.

"This business is over with, and there is nothing to worry about on that score," Kent thought. "But Barry is still missing, and if all this excitement didn't bring him back, there is something decidedly wrong!"

CHAPTER XXIV
At Grips with the Black Shadow

Unconscious of the events at the lodge, Barry crouched in the snow at the base of the quarry wall and gazed in the direction of the shed into which the figure in black had disappeared. His whole plan of action had to be changed, and for the time being he did not know what to do. He had planned to return to the tool house by way of the tunnel and tell his friends what he had discovered, but now it was highly dangerous to go back that way.

"The bale of hay sort of slides down on the trapdoor when you pull it down," he thought. "Perhaps he won't find out that someone has been in the passageway. I'm glad I closed all doors and walls behind me! But there may be footprints or something else to give me away. Gosh, this is a tough situation!"

The man in black was undoubtedly going to the lodge to start his series of annoyances, and Barry knew that these things would frighten the girls. Besides preventing that, he wanted more than anything else to take this prowler a captive, and if it was not done tonight, it might never be done. He fairly groaned as he saw the hopelessness of the situation.

"The boys may not get him, and if we lose him this time we're sunk! If I had my hunting rifle I'd go back along the tunnel and call on him to surrender, but I haven't a thing, and I imagine that the man is armed or at least able to put up a good fight. It would be suicide to follow him through the passageway. But I must get back!"

There were just two ways open to him: through the underground tunnel or by way of the woods. Of course the secret passage was the quickest route, but it was also the most dangerous. Barry decided not to risk it.

"It will take me a little longer to dash through the woods, but it will be a heap safer," he reflected. "If I went through the tunnel and met the spook face to face, I'd never be able to get away, and I've simply got to get back and warn the people at the lodge!"

Rising from his stooping position, Barry began to run toward the shed. He did not like the idea of having to pass it, for the man might have found out that someone had been in the passage, and might have returned to investigate the vicinity of the quarry. There was a chance that the black shadow might step out of the shed just as he passed, and if that happened things would not be well for the boy. But there was no help for it, and he sprinted past, glancing sideways in some alarm and ready to increase his speed if need be. The door of the shed, however, remained closed, and no one challenged him as he sped past.

"Good luck!" he exulted, as he left the quarry and plunged into the woods. "I made that all right, and now if I can get to the lodge just about as soon as he does, everything will be all right."

He did not take the exact path that he and Kent had taken on the night of the big storm, since they had gone in a roundabout way, but, relying on chance, he cut across the timber belt in a straight line, hoping that he was not making any mistake. Running was not easy because the snow was loose and the under snow had melted and then frozen again, making slippery footing. Occasionally his foot hit the root of a tree or a stone, and once he dropped on one knee and only saved himself from a complete fall by his outflung hands. But he struggled on, determined to reach the ones in the lodge as soon as possible.

When he reached the edge of the trees he saw the man in black sneaking from the tool house toward the rear porch of the lodge. At the same time something happened that caused the black shadow to stop and flatten himself against the wall of the house and made Barry halt in his run.

There was a sudden stir and some shouts, and then Coach Jordan and the other boys came running across the porch and jumped into the snow. Watching with bewildered eyes, Barry thought for a moment that they had somehow discovered the presence of the black shadow, but they did not come along the side of the lodge building, but dashed across the snow in the direction of the Bronson cabin. Barry followed them with his eyes, and then he noticed that the sleighs were gone. The situation began to dawn upon him.

"Somebody has taken the sleighs, and the boys are after them. Carter Wolf said he was going to do something to break up our party, and I guess he'll do it in one way or another. Some of those sleighs are borrowed, and I hope they don't smash them up in any way."

He wondered what the man in black would do and once more looked in his direction. The prowler had been as completely surprised as Barry had been, and while the boys were running he remained perfectly still, pressed close against the wall. But now he had glided in swift retreat to the back porch, which afforded more shelter.

There was another exodus from the lodge as the girls followed the boys, accompanied by the leaping, barking Castor Oil. Jennie had been feeding him marshmallows, and he was completely her slave, so much so that, when Charlie had run out, his clumsy animal companion had watched him go without any desire to follow him. He was content to run with the girls, dashing and barking in a wild display of good spirits.

Barry could hear the girls talking, and he watched them disappear down the slope that led from the front of the Bronson cabin to the lake. Something had happened down there, and he was anxious to know what it was, but his duty now was to watch the man who had taken refuge on the back porch of the hunting lodge. No doubt his plans had been upset as had Barry's, and it was interesting to see what he would do under the circumstances. Would he beat a retreat down the passageway and be lost to them, Barry wondered? Of course, if the man did, it would be much safer for them simply to get some officers of the law up there and try and trace the tunnel and find out where the man lived. But the thought did not satisfy him. He wanted to catch the prowler on the spot, so that he would have no loophole through which to escape when accused of causing the disturbances at Bluff Lodge.

Perhaps the shadow would go back into the tool house and wait until they got back, so as to produce rappings and noises. If this was his program, Barry felt sure that he could tackle the man on the spot and hold him until help arrived, but he would want that help to be pretty near at the time. No doubt the prowler was armed, as anyone engaged in a desperate business was likely to be, unless he had scorned to go armed against a group of high-school boys and girls.

141

Barry was not left long in doubt. The man had hesitated because he had been doing some rapid thinking, and at last he had made up his mind. Leaving the back porch, he ran hastily to the living-room window and peered in. Then he bent low to escape the light from the fire and the lamps and passed on to the front, where he crossed the porch and entered the front door.

Barry guessed his intention at once. The boys and girls had run out and left many things behind them, among other things some fairly good coats, and the pocketbooks of the girls were on the table. The black shadow had made up his mind to take them and get away, and perhaps to come back with his knocking pranks later on. Knowing the lodge as well as he seemed to, he would no doubt go out the back as they came in the front. Fate had put him in position to make a daring and completely successful raid.

Barry lost no time. Running his best, he left the timber and cut on a straight line for the lodge. He did not know what the boys were doing down there at the lake, and he had no time to go and find out. It was his supreme chance, and he had the feeling that if he lost out now, the ghostly prowler of Bluff Lodge would never be captured. He leaped to the porch and ran across it into the dark hall and finally jerked the door to the living room open, blinking in the light of the lamps as his eyes swept the interior of the place.

The tall man in the black overcoat, hat, and gloves whirled at the sound of his coming and turned two burning dark eyes upon him. But if Barry expected to see his face, he was disappointed. A black handkerchief obscured all of it except his eyes, which seemed to glare out above the covering. He had been feverishly picking up coats, hats, and pocketbooks and was in the act of taking a fur piece belonging to Mrs. Jordan when Barry burst into the room. As the boy faced him with resolute though pale face, the man pointed a black-gloved finger at him.

"Get out of here, boy!" he cried, hoarsely. "Get out or you'll wish you had!"

Barry had made up his mind, on the way, that talking would be a waste of time. From the moment that he had opened the door he was preparing for the struggle that was sure to come. He had opened his Mackinaw coat while running, and now he dropped it to the floor behind him. Then, even while the man was pointing at him, he leaped across the floor at the black-clad figure.

He was tense and his throat was dry as he closed in on the intruder. His great fear was that the man would draw a weapon and shoot him down. But the truth of the matter was that he had engaged the man at exactly the right time. The outlaw had his arms full of coats and other things, and as Barry grappled with him he was vainly trying to shake a pocketbook loose, the chain of which had become twisted around his middle finger on his right hand. This incident, small as it was, gave Barry a fighting chance.

His arms went around the man, and with a twist the high-school boy swept his adversary off his feet. They went down with a resounding crash to the floor, and the black hat rolled off, revealing a rather well-shaped head with a high forehead. The black eyes seemed to look into Barry's face for an instant in surprise.

Then their expression turned to one of deadly hate, and the battle was on. Only for a moment did the man accept his quick overthrow. In the twinkling of an eye he was fighting like a tiger, snarling exceedingly bad language as his eyes seemed to shoot out fire. Barry felt the muscles under the long black overcoat stiffen and become like steel, and the fingers that began to creep and grope for his throat were wiry and powerful. Reaching for one of the man's hands, Barry was tossed forward, and his arm brushed the black handkerchief from his face. Only for an instant did he see the features of his enemy. The man was about forty years old, with a thin face and small mustache. Just now the veins on his forehead stood out, and his teeth showed slightly as he exerted himself to overcome the mystery hunter.

The man launched a blow at Barry which caught him off guard and caused him to pause in his efforts to pin down the hands of the prowler. The fist of the stranger landed just under Barry's chin, and in the pain and surprise of it the boy hesitated. This was just what the man was waiting for. His long thin legs came up, one of them hooked over Barry's neck, and a mighty tug sent the boy tumbling backward.

Before the young mystery hunter could recover, the black shadow was upon him and strong fingers had gripped his throat, cutting off his wind instantly. Sudden fire and aching pain shot through the boy from Cloverfield.

"This is the end!" flashed through his bewildered mind. "I'm completely beaten!"

At that moment the twins came running in to get a blanket for Carter Wolf. They paused on the threshold and stared at the scene before them incredulously.

CHAPTER XXV
The Mystery of the Lodge

The Ford boys stood in the doorway and gazed at the unexpected sight before them like persons in a daze. The fingers of the man were clutching Barry's throat, and one knee was planted with crushing force on his chest. The face which the stranger turned toward the twins was dark with rage and exertion, and his black eyes were fierce and defiant. So utterly unexpected was this scene to the two newcomers that they remained rooted to the spot until a choking cry burst from Barry, who was looking at them imploringly.

Then Mac suddenly came to life, and a growl of anger burst from him. "Come on, Tim," he shouted. "This man is killing Barry!"

"Keep off!" snarled the man, half turning to face them. "I'm going away from here, and nobody is going to stop me! Keep away, or I'll——"

The last part of his sentence was never finished. Mac hurled himself on the stranger, jerking his hands away from Barry's throat. Tim joined him with vigor, and they fairly tore him off of their chum. He came up with a spring and wrapped his arms around the twins, twisting them roughly in an effort to break away. He realized that others were coming, and his one desire now was to thrust them aside and get away.

But the Ford boys had no intention of letting him go, and even Barry, weak and shaken as he was, returned to the fight to keep the man from escaping. Catching him around one leg, Barry held him tightly while the twins tried to break loose from his iron grip, at the same time striving to throw him. Back and forth they swayed and struggled, panting and straining. The center table was pushed to one side, and they were up against a wicker chair when the others came back.

They had been coming along slowly with Carter Wolf, and could not understand why the twins did not hasten with the blanket. The lodge prowler heard them coming, and the perspiration of a real fear now stood out on his head. Like a wild animal trapped, he looked around, and just as the incoming party filled the doorway and gazed in wonder at the struggle, he drew back his free foot and prepared to deal Barry a kick that would free the leg that the boy was holding. He felt that if he could once get that leg loose he could drag the twins into the hall leading to the lodge kitchen and somehow get rid of them.

But in raising his other foot he lost his balance, and he and the twins went down in a crashing heap, breaking the wicker chair to bits. Screams came from the girls, and the coach and Kent leaped forward to pull the combatants apart. Carter Wolf forgot his forlorn condition, and his friends stared in amazement. The coats and pocketbooks on the floor, the table back against the wall, and the general signs of confusion put them all at a loss.

"Here, what is going on here?" Coach Jordan asked, as he hauled the twins off of the fallen man. But to his astonishment Kent immediately threw himself on the stranger, holding his hands out in front of him by the wrists.

"Get a rope or a curtain cord or something," Kent commanded, and Tim turned to look for something. But at the same moment the black shadow suddenly tried a dash for the hall door. Instantly all four boys, including the bruised Barry, leaped at him and bore him to the floor. The girls again screamed, and the coach looked bewildered. The captive addressed him.

"Call these fool boys off, Jordan! You know me!"

"Who is he?" Barry asked, finding his voice hoarse.

"Why, this is Felix Morganson, nephew of the lady who owns this lodge!" was the unexpected reply.

"What!" cried the mystery hunters, in chorus.

146

"Yes, I am, and when my aunt hears of this, you'll hear a thing or two," said Felix Morganson. But the boys were not at all worried.

"That's all right," said Kent, warmly. "But you are the ghost of this so-called haunted lodge."

"Yes, he is," nodded Barry. "I saw him come up here through a secret underground tunnel, and when I arrived on the scene in this room he was stealing our coats and everything else in sight."

"That's a lie!" denied the prisoner, his keen eyes shifting around.

"It isn't, and if we hadn't come along when we did, you would have just about killed Barry," Mac declared. By this time Tim had found a rope, and Kent took it and tried to tie the wrists of the prisoner behind him. Felix Morganson looked at the coach.

"Jordan, are you going to stand for this?" he shouted. "Somebody will get into big trouble, and you are in charge of these boys!"

The coach hesitated, plainly at a loss, and Barry quickly took command of the situation. "It's all right, Mr. Jordan, and I will assume full responsibility. My father has been trying for a long time to find the man who has been giving this lodge the reputation of being haunted, and Mr. Morganson is the one who did the rapping and thumping. We must not let him get away."

Before the athletic director could speak, there was a knock on the door of the lodge. They looked at one another with wondering glances, and then Charlie Black hurried to the door. One of the girls swiftly wrapped a blanket around Carter Wolf and pushed him over in front of the fire. Kent and Barry kept their eyes on Morganson.

Charlie returned with strange companions. Two men with police stars on their coats came in, driving the French couple before them. One of the men held the Frenchman's gun in the crook of his arm. Pierre and his wife looked sullen.

"Evening, folks!" nodded the stouter of the two men. "I'm Sheriff Paulson, and this is McHenry. We've been keepin' watch on these Frenchies for a few days, and just now they was outside of this window, gettin' ready to shoot the lamps out." He looked at Felix Morganson with interest. "So here you are, Mr. Morganson! You ain't in Canada or South America!"

"I think he's been here all along, Sheriff," Barry spoke up. "I found a secret tunnel from that quarry over there to the tool house out back. He is the one who has been giving the place a bad name."

"Found a tunnel, did you?" the sheriff asked, looking at Barry with interest. "There used to be some counterfeiters operating around here, in an old cabin that stood where this lodge is, and I guess they was the ones used it. So Mr. Morganson has been hauntin' his own aunt's property! These Frenchies have been helpin' him right along, and I guess squeezin' plenty of money out of him."

Barry suddenly remembered something. "Which one of you shot at Wolf and his friends the night they sat on the front porch?" he asked.

"I try scare heem away," the Frenchman admitted.

After some further conversation the sheriff agreed to take Morganson to his aunt in Cloverfield. The would-be ghost of the lodge insisted upon seeing her, and so at last he and his French allies went off with the two county officials. Jordan, Bill Jefferson, and Tom Bailey hitched up a sleigh and drove them to Fox Point, where the sheriff took Morganson and the woodsman and his wife on to Cloverfield in his own conveyance.

The boys from Rake Island did not stay long after the sheriff left. Carter Wolf thanked everybody with averted eyes and went off with his friends, who dragged the sleighs back to the lake bank before disappearing. In the morning it was an easy task for the boys to pull them on up the slope and hitch up the horses.

Barry was somewhat mussed up and quite sore, but he was the hero of the hour. They sat around the living-room fire and listened with rapt attention while he told of his trip along the tunnel, and when Coach Jordan and the others came back, it had to be told all over again. They sat up until late in the night excitedly discussing the events of the evening.

"But we still do not know why Morganson pretended to be kidnaped and then hung around haunting the place," Tim reminded them.

"I have an idea, from some things that he admitted to Sheriff Paulson, that he did it to knock down the value of the place and buy it from his aunt for a mere song," spoke up the coach. "He always had a perfect passion for the lodge and was determined to have it by fair means or foul. I believe that he was trying to buy it through Brand Curry."

In this Coach Jordan was correct. Felix Morganson had always had a great longing to own Bluff Lodge, and with Brand Curry and his French friends he had planned to ruin the reputation of the place and have his friend buy it very cheaply. Until Mrs. Morganson died, Brand Curry would continue to own the property, as far as outward appearances were concerned, and then Felix would take it over when his indulgent aunt passed away. So he had acted a false kidnaping part and had lived in a small cabin down in the hollow of a mountain spur close to the abandoned quarry.

With the capture of Felix Morganson, all mysteries were cleared up. He was the one who had taken their sled and who had dropped the snow behind the chimney upstairs in the hunting lodge. Having a key to the lodge, he entered it at will. The Frenchman and his wife had been writing to him for money, and as he did not send them any, they came in person to collect it and he joined them at Fox Point. Officers of the law had become suspicious and had trailed the French couple.

The young people at the lodge were eager to explore the counterfeiters' tunnel that night, but Barry persuaded them to wait until the following day, and they finally consented. Early the next morning they traversed it and enjoyed the experience. When the story finally got out, many came to see it.

Felix Morganson had an interview with his aunt, and the general opinion was that she was too easy with him, for he disappeared shortly afterward, and no charges of any kind were ever placed against him. The French couple also vanished and were never seen in that part of the country again.

When the young people from the Cloverfield High School drove away from Bluff Lodge on the morning after the capture of the black shadow, they all agreed that it had been an exciting and enjoyable straw ride. Barry, Mac, Pearl, and Charlie rode on the foremost sleigh, and Kent and the twins were directly behind them. Castor Oil still clung to the girl who had satisfied his sweet tooth.

"Now you boys have certainly earned the name of 'mystery hunters,'" Pearl said, as the sleigh glided on toward home. "We're all proud of you."

Mac grinned. "We've passed our first test in mysteries! Wait until the next one comes along!" Just as the sleigh entered the timber, Barry turned to look back at the log building. "So long, old haunted lodge!" he smiled. "You are going to be mighty lonesome for your friend the black shadow!"

THE END